THE CAMIGAS SCARF

THE CAMIGAS SCARF

Mother

BOOK ONE

ALDER ALLENSWORTH

Edited by Robin Cain.
Cover illustration by Nupu Press.
www.nupupress.com

Copyright © 2024 Alder Allensworth
www.alderallensworth.com

ISBN: 979-8-9900189-0-7
1st printing 2024

This book is dedicated to the Camigas,
women who support women on the Camino de Santiago.

ACKNOWLEDGMENTS

My gratitude goes out to the Camino de Santiago, the people of Spain, and people worldwide who support and maintain this magical place where the impossible becomes possible.

To Gigi Mashburn, finder of the scarf. She embodies the spirit of sisterhood, Listening to the scarf, she blessed it and sent it on its way. To Annie Herman for showing me the purpose of the scarf. And to every scarf carrier and all the women who choose to walk the Camino.

To Lorena Gaibor, Caroline Loder, and Jenna D'Amore who created and maintain a safe, supportive place for women who walk the Camino with the Facebook page *Camigas – A Buddy System for Women on the Camino*, and for graciously permitting me to use the name The Camigas Scarf.

I especially want to thank Jenna McKenna who read the rough draft and encouraged me to give voice to the scarf and passion to my characters. She is the glue that holds the Tampa Writers Alliance together, whose members month after month read my drafts, gently taught me writing techniques, and cheered me on when I wanted to give up.

I am honored to have the beta readers Chris Myers, Shoshana Kerewsky, and Shawn Buller who taught me about voice, made wonderful suggestions, and encouraged me to believe in the work.

My mentor Beebe Bahrami whose knowledge of the Camino and the sacred feminine guided me along the way. I leaned hard on her Moon guide of the Camino de Santiago. I used her book to fact-check the places I visited and the legends of the Frances Route.

I would have been lost without John Brierly's A Pilgrim's Guide to the Camino de Santiago: St. Jean – Roncevalles – Santiago.

Not just women have touched this book, Ron Angst read the first complete draft, corrected my punctuation, and my memory of key places along the way.

Three women jumped in to make this book possible, to bring it to life when I was at my lowest: Robin Cain for her astute suggestions and final editing; Kim from The Stone Boat in Rabanal del Camino for the beautiful layout, and artist and *peregrina,* Nupu, for this charming cover illustration.

To my husband Ben Ritter who supports my dream of making this trilogy a reality and cheers me on when I walk the Camino de Santiago.

And most importantly, *the scarf...*

Introduction

Love like the Mother
Dance like the Maiden
Think like the Crone

- Stenciled on a jar of homemade Sangria
that was given to me by a wise crone.

The Camigas scarf has been passed from Camiga to Camiga in solidarity with their pilgrimages. A Camiga is a term coined in 2015 when a few women got together to support women on the Camino. 'Ca' stands for Camino, and in Spanish, 'amiga' - for female friends.

The Camino de Santiago is one of the few places in the world where a woman can go, walk alone on pilgrimage and feel safe. In March of 2015, the unthinkable happened. A young woman was assaulted and murdered. The perpetrator was found and convicted. The *'Camigas-A Buddy System for Women on the Camino'* Facebook page was created so women who want to participate in the pilgrimage have a safe place to connect with other women and plan their Caminos. At this writing, the Facebook page has almost 32,000 members.

I have so much gratitude for Lorena Gaibor, Caroline Loder, and Jenna D'Amore for seeing the need women have for a buddy to embark upon such an arduous pilgrimage. They have given me their blessing to use the term 'Camiga.'

The origin of the scarf goes back a little bit further. The story starts in 2010 when Gigi walked the Camino Frances from St. Jean Pied de Port, France to Santiago de Compostela, Spain. Along the way, she met a young American woman in a small town who was working in Spain as an au pair. The young woman was so happy to hear English being spoken she joined them for the evening. She missed the last bus back to her employer's house, but Gigi made sure she had a safe place to stay. The next morning, she left early to catch the bus and left her scarf behind. Gigi rescued the scarf and carried it with her, hoping to connect with the young woman again, but unfortunately, this never happened.

Fast forward seven years to the fall of 2017 when I was getting ready to walk my Camino. I worked with Gigi and asked her if we could have lunch. I wanted to learn all I could about the Camino before I left. Gigi brought me three gifts: a palm frond cross that had been blessed, four Euros to buy a cup of cafe con leche, and the scarf.

As Gigi was preparing for our luncheon, she opened the drawer where she kept her Camino and hiking clothes. In the back of the drawer was the scarf. She pulled it out and, as she stroked its soft fibers, memories of her Camino came flooding back. She got the distinct feeling that it needed to go back to the Camino, but she didn't know why. She knew she had to give it to me to take back.

Gigi has the reputation of being 'connected' to a higher power. I was not going to question her wisdom. I took the scarf and completed the entire five hundred miles of the Camino Frances *(the Way)* with it around my neck in October and November of 2017. I appreciated the warmth of the scarf as fall turned into winter. The Camino wasn't easy, but knowing I had the support of the other Camigas, Gigi, and the scarf, I made it to Santiago.

Annie, a woman from my local area, saw me posting about my Camino on the Camigas Facebook page. She messaged me and asked me to meet her for lunch and to assist her in preparing for her Camino. I took my pack loaded with everything I had carried. Sharing the contents, item by item, I reminded her that less is better since she would have to have to carry its weight across Spain.

I pulled out the scarf and told her its story. She leaned in and met my gaze, it was written all over her face that she wanted to take the scarf back to the Camino. Reluctantly, I offered her the scarf. She accepted immediately. It was hard releasing this bit of yarn. The scarf served me well. It was around my neck the morning I walked into the square in front of the Cathedral in Santiago, completing my 500-mile Camino. The scarf had been my constant companion and support. It held all the fun memories and the hardships. But what was I going to do with a scarf in Florida? So, I handed it over.

It was wonderful to follow Annie and the scarf on her Camino. I cheered her on from the power of the internet. Seeing the pictures of her standing in front of the cathedral in Santiago wearing the scarf, I knew it had found its purpose, and why it had to go back to the Camino.

Annie's friend Donna was getting ready to walk the next year and Annie passed the scarf on to her. As of this writing, the scarf has accompanied Camigas on eleven Caminos. Each Camiga passes the scarf on to a woman who has been called to walk one of the ancient paths to Santiago, continuing a tradition of support for women and pilgrimage.

The Camigas Scarf Trilogy follows the journey of three women: a mother, a maiden, and a crone. Each character is fictional as I could not do justice to the experiences of the Camigas who have carried the scarf. I did not want to intrude upon the scarf carriers' personal reasons for walking the Camino.

Women of all ages and backgrounds walk the Camino for a variety of reasons. The Camino is a place of reflection and growth. The experiences of each character in the book were created in my imagination and consolidated from my interviews of women on the Camino, reading stories, Facebook posts, and my own Camino experiences. Any similarity to a real person is just a coincidence.

Each book highlights a different Camino route. The historic places each woman experiences are authentic to that particular route. I have taken care to research each route, as well as having walked them myself. Some of the albergues have changed their names and owners and may not be found on the Camino today.

Book One – join Helen, the mother, as she embarks upon a life-changing pilgrimage, starting in St. Jean Pied de Port, struggling across the Pyrenees to Santiago de Compostela, to discover a light within herself.

Book Two – Valerie, the maiden takes her broken heart to Spain and unexpectedly finds herself on Camino Norte. Taking a fortuitous detour across the mountains of the Camino Primitive to Santiago de Compostela heals her heart and her soul.

Book Three – Dorothy, our crone, wearied by life's responsibilities, wanders alone up the west coast of Portugal to Santiago de Compostela, much to the dismay of her adult children, and becomes renewed.

Thank you for following the journey of the scarf. It is my wish that if you have never walked a Camino, you will one day consider making this life-changing pilgrimage.

- Alder

CHAPTER I

MADRID, SPAIN

"I've heeded the call to walk to Santiago." I shrugged, smiling with disconcertment. "Actually, it's a mother-daughter trip to celebrate Hannah's graduation from high school."

"Whatever the reason, I'm so glad you're finally doing it." Mary jumped out of her chair and enveloped me in one of her famous hugs. She had saved us a sweet table in a private corner of the tearoom, one with a candy-striped pink tablecloth, lace-edged napkins, and real china cups and plates. I loved this place.

Mary had walked the Camino de Santiago, alone, about seven years prior. She and I had been in nursing school together. While she went on to get her PhD and teach nursing, I got my Mrs. instead.

"Helen, I brought you some things you need for your Camino. Here's four euros. Buy yourself a cup of cafe con leche, on me. It's out of this world. This is a cross made of a palm frond I got for you on Palm Sunday. It's been blessed and doesn't weigh anything, and this, well..."

Mary got a distant look in her eyes, and a smile started to play about her lips. "This scarf must go back to the Camino. I don't know why. It just does. It's probably a God thing. I was looking for my pareo when I found the scarf shoved in the back of my bottom drawer. Never found the pareo. I pulled the scarf out of the drawer and stroked the softness of the wool; it spoke to me. You must take it back to Spain."

"Wow, thank you." I took a sip of Earl Grey tea and put clotted cream on my scone.

"I was in Estella with my walking buddy, —loved Estella— and this young girl walked up to us. In a shy voice she said, 'Hi.' I could tell she was an American right away. But she didn't have on all the trappings of a pilgrim, and she smelled better, too." Mary laughed as she told the story. "She looked so lost. I invited her to join us for dinner and before we knew it, she had missed her bus back to Pamplona."

"Oh my, what happened?"

"There was no way I was going to let her sit in a bus station all night, so we snuck her into our albergue. Turns out she was an au pair and wanted to see the world, but all she had seen so far were a bunch of bratty kids. But, hey, she was going for it."

"How old was she?" I asked, thinking about Hannah.

"I believe she said nineteen and that she was from some small town in the Carolinas."

"She must have been so lonely for home," I said.

"But when I got up the next morning, she was gone. Her scarf was draped over the end of her bed. I tried to find her, but she'd just disappeared. I put the word out on the pilgrims' grapevine but never found her. So, you see, it must go back to Spain...

The tone for the fasten seat belt sign wakes me from my reverie. I take the scarf from behind my head, unfold it, and put it around my neck, then check to see if my seat belt is fastened. Glancing at Hannah's lap, I see she is ready for landing, too.

"Mom. I'm an adult, I believe I can handle it." Hannah says, rolling her eyes.

"I know, but I'll never stop being your mother."

"Spain. We have been talking about and training for this trip forever. I remember thinking it was lame doing a mother-daughter trip, but then you threw in Spain which took it up a notch," Hannah says. "So, have you set an intention for the trip?"

"An intention?" I fiddle with the fringe of the scarf around my neck.

"Yeah, you know, like Sister Sophia suggested."

"Alright. My intention is to make a wonderful memory with you, so when you go to college in the fall, graduate, get married, and have children of your own, you can look back on this special time we had together."

"Whoa, don't get me married off so fast. That was okay for you, but it's not what I want. I know you want grandchildren, but I have a few plans of my own first."

I try to be calm I know she's baiting me and it's going to be a long trip.

"So, what's your intention?" I ask.

"Hm, I'm not totally sure." She pulls her long braid from behind her back and starts looking for split ends. "But I want adventure in my life. I want to explore the world."

The plane lands with a jolt, and I throw my arm across her chest. Hannah looks at me and starts laughing. "Oh, Mom, do you really think that would've kept me safe?"

"You'll understand when you have children of your own."

We get up and take our packs from the overhead compartment. This is all the luggage we're allowed to bring and I've no idea how we're going to survive in Spain for six weeks with the few things in our packs. I put my pack on my back and turn to Hannah. "Do you need help with yours?"

"I got it, Mom."

And she does. The pack looks like it belongs on her back, easily fitting her torso. Her thick curly auburn hair is tamed

4

into a plait down her back. I remember when my hair was that length. It was my best feature. But I cut it short long ago and let the gray start to streak it. Silver among the gold, my husband Ken always says. My eyes match my hair, a reddish brown. When we first married, Ken used to say that he could get lost in the color of my eyes.

I wonder how he's doing and if he misses us. He's probably exhausted from a long day of surgery and then has to pick up the twins from their Mimi and Papa's house. At least I know Mimi will make sure they all get fed. Those boys can eat. I don't know where they put it. Like Ken, not an ounce of fat. Pregnancy played havoc with my figure. I used to look pretty good in a bikini, but that was a long time ago, and having them was worth it.

I look at Hannah leading us through the airport. She's blossomed into a beautiful young woman with the same long legs and flat stomach I had at her age. She has her father's baby-blue eyes though. Boys are going to be drawn to her like bears to honey. I don't wish she was ugly or fat. Ugly and fat never protected a woman from unwanted advances anyway. She doesn't understand how vulnerable a woman can be. This will be her first foray into the world, at least she has a safety net of women to guide her. I don't want her walking through the world in fear, but I do want her safe.

We make our way down to baggage claim where Sister Sophia is meeting us. Not that we have any more baggage to pick up. Sister has been very firm about what we're allowed to bring, assuring us we could purchase anything extra we may need along the way. Hannah seems to relish the idea of minimalism, always talking about low impact on the earth. Our generation was about collecting more to leave to our children, and they want less.

"Hey Mom, look, that must be our group."

Sister Sophia is holding a sign, standing beside two other ladies in hiking gear. Finding her so easily is a relief.

Sister's iron-grey hair peeks out from under her veil. She has a fine nose and full lips, but her best feature is her sparkling expressive blue eyes. When she smiles in greeting, her warmth and confidence radiate out and envelopes us. I can detect fine lines starting to etch into her features which add maturity to a beautiful face. Below the hem of her habit, a pair of well-worn hiking boots adorn her feet. Hannah, seeing my gaze, elbows me and whispers, "This woman is the real deal."

"Welcome to Spain," Sister Sophia says.

"Oh, thank you, Sister. It's such a blessing to be here."

"I'd like to introduce you to Camille from Missouri and Emily from Seattle. This is Helen and her daughter Hannah from Florida."

"Pleased to meet you all," I say, as I take in Emily's long muscular legs emerging from under her hiking skirt. Her dark skin seems to scarcely contain the power in her calves. There isn't even a hint of a muffin top where her hiking skirt meets her fitted technical top. The only thing that might betray her age are the curly grey streaks pushing their way through her closely cropped black hair, and the lines at the side of her eyes as she smiles her greeting.

I compare her body to my frumpy middle-aged one, with my baggy shirt covering all sorts of sins. However, I do believe my legs still look pretty good from all the walking I do.

Camille's hair is an iron grey, controlled in a bun at the nape of her neck. There's a warmth emanating from her brown eyes, and she has a welcoming smile. I can see the no-nonsense Midwestern-ness etched in her features. She's wearing stretch pants, a tunic top, and sensible hiking shoes. Her sturdy body looks like she has spent her life working on a farm.

Oh my, how am I ever going to keep up with these women?

Just then, another woman appears. "Howdy y'all, I'm Jackie from Abilene.

"Texas, right?" Hannah says and we all laugh.

"I reckon you two peas in a pod are related, with that curly red hair. I would kill for hair like that."

There are five of us now. Five women walking alone across Spain, with a nun for protection. I sure hope she has an inside track to God. We quickly gather ourselves and follow Sister Sophia, hurrying to keep up with her quick strides.

Am I going to have to keep up with this pace all the way across Spain?

We finally reach the small van.

CHAPTER 2

MADRID TO ST. JEAN PIED DE PORT, FRANCE

Sister Sophia opens the back of the van and our packs easily fit inside. We each get a seat and settle down for the six-hour drive to St. Jean-Pied-de-Port, our starting point of the Camino Frances on the French side of the Pyrenees.

"Please bow your heads," commands Sister Sophia. "Oh God, who brought your servant Abraham out of the Chaldeans, protecting him in his wanderings, and who guided the Hebrew people across the desert, we ask that you watch over us, your servants, as we walk in the love of your name to Santiago de Compostela."

"Oh, Sister, what a beautiful prayer," Emily says.

"It's an ancient prayer usually given at the end of the Pilgrims' Mass. You will hear it many times on this trip. This is not a vacation in Spain. This is a pilgrimage. There will be many hardships and lessons along the way."

Hannah turns to me and mouths, "What have you gotten us into?"

I pat her on the leg and reassure her that it can't be that bad. But after that prayer, I have my reservations but I'm not about to let Hannah see my concern. She will need my strength.

Jackie pulls out her cell phone and begins to speak quietly to her family back home. I pull out mine to let Ken know we've arrived safely. I decide to just text him as we seem to communicate best this way. Due to his thoughtfulness, I have an international calling plan which I know wasn't cheap. But Ken never scrimps on safety.

"Look, the Pyrenees," Sister says when the mountain range comes into view. "We will walk up into these mountains tomorrow." This breaks us out of our jet lag reverie. They are much bigger than I imagined. The van starts to chug up the winding road. I realize this isn't going to be easy.

My phone dings with a text back from Ken. *Glad UR safe, have fun.* Brief as usual.

Camille says she heard Sister Sophia speak at her church in Kansas City and was called to walk the Camino. When Sister visited our parish in St. Petersburg, I felt the same calling. Camille goes on to say that she is a widow and an empty nester. Her four sons are grown with wives of their own and grandchildren along the way.

Emily tells us that she is taking a leave of absence from her job as a project manager at a high-tech company. She hopes to renew her faith.

Jackie shares that she lives in Dallas and is married. She has one daughter, like me. She chokes a bit on her words.

"We so wanted more children, but it wasn't in God's plan. We tried and tried, but I finally decided to be content with what I had. My husband and I put our energy into giving to others instead. But that doesn't mean we quit trying," she adds with a wink.

She is very blonde, and I'm tempted to ask if it is natural. Despite hours of travel, her make-up and hair are perfect. She looks more prepared for a cruise than a pilgrimage. She could be somewhere between late 30's and early 50's, but it's hard to tell. When she begins talking about her faith and the Camino her conviction draws me in. What a strange group the Camino has called.

What do I believe? I was brought up in the Catholic church and married a Catholic. We vowed to bring up our children in the faith. Every Sunday, I show up early to prepare the altar for the service. Ken and I assist with the parish nurse program, watching after the sick and elderly. This is part of our faith and our tradition.

I loved learning about the angels and saints in CCD (the Confraternity of Christian Doctrine). And I've always wanted an experience like Sister Bernadette who saw the Virgin Mary. She stood by her faith, and Lourdes has since become a place of healing. But this is all past history.

Nothing like that happens today. Today, we would call her beliefs psychosis and give her a pill. I've always wondered what it would be like to hear the voices of the saints.

My ears pop as we make our way higher into the mountains. There are a few red-topped barns and pastures peeking out from the lush green forest. Storm clouds race across the sky, leaving a fresh-washed appearance to the land in their wake —and a slick road. As we continue to climb on the narrow winding mountain roads, little shrines on posts decorated with fresh flowers come into view.

"Sister, what are these shrines?" I ask.

"Oh, memorials to people killed on these roads. They get treacherous in storms and fog," she says nonchalantly. I grip the armrest as if that is going to keep us from sliding off the mountain. I pray the driver knows what he's doing. I wouldn't want another little shrine erected in our memory on the side of the road, so people could just shake their heads and cross themselves in gratitude that it wasn't them.

The sun bursts out from behind a cloud and the vista it illuminates is awe-inspiring. A checkerboard of farms, fields, and trees funneling down into valleys. The low stone fences give definition to the land. Around the next bend, we reach the summit. It is strewn with boulders and there are winding dirt paths making their way through the maze.

OMG, we are going to be crossing this tomorrow!

This makes the stairs in the parking garage look like child's play. I fondle the fringe of the scarf around my neck, remembering that Mary had confidence in me. I am going to have to call upon this strength daily.

I don't have long to contemplate this thought as I hear Sister say, "Welcome to France." I didn't even realize we crossed the border. There is no wall or guard house here as we start back down into the valley formed by the Nive River.

Sister tells us about the history of St. Jean, how it was a commerce crossroads as early as the 12th century, at the foot of the pass into the Pyrenees. It's protected by a wall encircling the town, but that didn't stop Richard the Lion Heart from burning it down. It was rebuilt by the Kings of Navarre. Navarre is a region that overlaps Spain and France, but the boundaries are surely blurred.

"That's so dope," Hannah says, as she drinks in every word. I look at her in surprise. I had no idea she was interested in history.

We drive up a narrow street and come to a stop beside the gate of La-Porte-Saint-Jean.

"We get out here," Sister Sophia says, tucking a stray curl under her veil. "We're not allowed to drive through the gate. The streets are made of bricks and too small for car traffic. We like to preserve the old parts of our cities. Grab your packs and let's go."

The open gate is fashioned in an arch, with stone walls abutting it. I bet there was a big wooden door here back in the day, protecting the city. I can just see the gatekeeper opening a peephole, like in *The Wizard of Oz,* to determine if we are worthy of entering his city.

As we exit the car, a shiver goes down my spine. At 545 feet above sea level and on the same latitude as New York, what did I expect? The middle of May is still winter in New York as far as I'm concerned. I wrap the scarf close around my neck to keep out the cold wind as it funnels down the mountains into the valley. The soft wool protected Mary on her pilgrimage. Maybe it will do the same for me.

We grab our packs and catch up with Sister as she strides down the narrow brick street to our *gite*. Sister told us that the pilgrims' lodging in France is termed gite. In Spain, they are called *alburgues*.

The uneven bricks test my footing as I try to adjust my pack to sit more firmly on my hips. Sister Sophia turns to her left and knocks on the red wooden door of the gite. There, next to the door, hangs a pair of old boots filled with red geraniums. A man answers the knock.

"Peter, how are you?" Sister Sophia says.

"Ah, Sister Sophia, welcome back. And ladies, welcome to France," he replies in perfect English with a rich French accent.

We follow Sister's lead and put our hiking poles in a large clay vessel by the front door, then sit on the bench and remove our boots. Peter calls our names after he checks in Camille. She and Sister make their way up the stairs to our room. I stumble over my boots to Peter's desk.

"Ah, Florida," Peter exclaims. "Micky Mouse. You may find this pilgrimage to be a whole different experience. And you are the daughter, Hannah?" He makes note of our passport numbers and puts the first stamps on our pilgrim's credential.

The credential, our pilgrims' passport to the Camino, allows us to sleep in albergues and will document that we actually walked all the way across Spain to Santiago de Compostela. There, I will receive my certificate of completion called a Compostela, stating my accomplishment and the absolution of my sins—though I'm not sure what my sins are. I've led quite a normal life, I'm a good wife and mother, and though I've told the infrequent white lie, it was warranted at the time.

Hannah and I mount the stairs to our room which contains six bunk beds. Sister Sophia offers to take a top bunk and sets her pack on the floor next to the bed. Hannah follows suit and stakes out the top bunk by the window. I take the bunk beneath. Jackie puts her pack on the bed under Sister's. Sister stops her, telling her the pack must go on the floor to prevent vermin from getting on the bed.

"Vermin?" Camille exclaims as Emily enters the room.

"Well, bed bugs. In Spain, we call them *chinches*. They are known to travel in people's packs and on their bedding. Keeping things as clean as possible is very important. It's a rule of the Camino to never put your backpack on your bed. I have never had an issue and I don't want to start now. I always check the mattress before I stay in a gite, but I know Peter has never had a problem."

Jackie's pack hits the floor with a heavy *clunk*.

"What's in your pack?" Sister Sophia asks. "You know you'll have to carry it all the way to Santiago. Every ounce counts."

"Just my face," Jackie answers.

Hannah catches my eye and I give her the stink eye, that look of 'don't you dare,' while trying to contain my laughter. It must be the jet lag.

Jackie turns to Sister Sophia. "I don't go anywhere without my face."

I just can't contain my giggle any longer. Camille and Sister look at me in horror, but Jackie hoots and we all dissolve into laughter.

"Come on ladies, we must get across the street and register," Sister Sophia says with a smile.

I follow her out of the room, with one last look of longing at the bed. So much for an afternoon nap.

The volunteers in the Pilgrim's Office put our names in the register and a stamp on our credentials. We each buy a scallop shell for our packs and are provided with a weather report and map of the first leg of the trip. Sister Sophia had already arranged for us to stay at Orisson tomorrow night, 7.8 kilometers or just under five miles straight up the Pyrenees, and an altitude gain of about 3,000 feet. I've walked much further than that in training. And the stairs in the parking garage made a difference in my breathing. This shouldn't be a problem.

CHAPTER 3

ST. JEAN PIED DE PORT, FRANCE

Back at the gite. Camille has chosen the bunk beside mine. She apologizes in advance for any snoring, I show her my earplugs and smile.

I head to the bathroom and freshen up. Then go downstairs to the dining room, leaving Hannah resting on her bunk, reading our guidebook. Dishes and utensils are piled up on one of the two picnic tables covered with red checkered tablecloths. Sister puts me to work setting the table.

Peter comes in bearing wine and places a bottle on each table. A nice-looking couple joins us and introduces themselves. They are from France and have just arrived on foot. They began walking in Vezelay and had already walked over five hundred miles. They have chosen to finish their Camino here. Oh, my goodness, they look so fresh. Will I look that good when I reach Santiago?

A knock comes from the front door, and Peter welcomes another pilgrim, who is audibly sobbing. I go toward the lobby to offer assistance as he ushers her into the dining room. He introduces her as Tora from New Zealand and nods at me to assist her.

"Tora, what's wrong?" She can't be much older than Hannah, and she is all alone.

"Tired," she chokes out, trying to get herself together as more pilgrims arrive.

"What can I do to help?" I ask, but she just shakes her head.

I hand her the napkins to fold and put at each place. If she wants to talk later, I'll make myself available.

Next through the door is a family from South Korea. The parents are young, and the boy and girl are preteens. How they can afford to do this and why aren't the children in school?

A warm hearty voice, speaking French, comes from the lobby. He's asking about dinner. I can still remember some of my high school French. This may come in handy. He introduces himself as Karl from Germany and comes in with Juan from Portugal. So many names to remember.

We all take our seats and Peter pours us an aperitif. After passing the tray of glasses around, we toast the Camino. Peter asks each of us to share a little about ourselves and our intention for the pilgrimage. My mind goes blank. What can I say in front of a room of strangers?

"Hi, Emily from Seattle," she emits a confident smile. "Sister Sophia contacted my church to let us know about the pilgrimage. I applied for a spot and was accepted. I've been in the tech field for about twenty years. Even though it's made me a good living, there's more to life. I've lost the spirit and mystery of faith. Many women feel as though the Catholic church has abandoned them and they're correct. It's a patriarchal system and we need to restore the balance. My duty as a Christian and a woman is to be part of restoring that balance. I hope to develop a deeper faith and bring more young women back to the church."

Oh my. How am I ever going to keep up with this woman?

"Hi, Jackie from Texas, and I'm so tickled to be here with y'all. This is a dream come true for me. I've wanted to walk the Camino ever since I was little. My mother's from Spain, God rest her soul, and she brought me up on it. She married my father who was in the Navy, and they settled in Abilene after they retired. Daddy passed last Christmas. When Sister Sophia came to speak to our church, the coincidence was too much. I just had to come." She pauses and adds, "I'm here for absolution."

Hmm, wonder what she has to be absolved from?

Hannah elbows me under the table. I gave her the 'stink eye.' This is going to be a long trip.

Tora went next. "I flew from New Zealand, with three layovers, to Paris. When I arrived in Paris and went to baggage claim, my pack wasn't there. The airline made me check it because it contains my hiking poles," she chokes back a sob, "I don't know what to do. Everything is in my pack, except this fanny pack with my documents." Tears started rolling down her cheeks. "I had to catch the train to St. Jean. The customs agent at the airport was very nice and took my information. He said they'd track my pack down and send it to me."

"Honey, we look to be about the same size, I have a couple of extra things you can borrow until your pack arrives," Jackie says.

"There is a closet full of supplies here as many pilgrims donate gear, they don't want to carry over the Pyrenees," Peter says. "We'll make sure you are clothed and fed."

A look of gratitude washes over Tora's face.

Karl was next. He said, says that he walked out of his front door in Munich two weeks after his wife died of cancer and has not stopped. He's been on the Way for close to four months. He pours a glass of wine from the bottle on the table and takes a swig. "I still miss her, and I'm not going to stop walking. I cannot bear to go back home." He looks at me.

"I'm so sorry for your loss." I think about Ken, he's a constant. Could I make it on my own without him?

"I guess I'm next. I'm a housewife and my husband still works. He's a surgeon very dedicated to his patients.

Hannah's our oldest and she just graduated from high school. The boys, twins, will be juniors next fall. Sister Sophia spoke at our church in St. Petersburg, Florida. She said the Camino experience may deepen our relationship with God and provide divine direction in our lives. I had to come. Since Hannah was graduating from high school, I thought it would be the perfect mother-daughter experience before she heads off to college, and maybe just the thing Hannah needs to give direction to her future." I nod to Hannah, who is rolling her eyes at me.

"Mom and I were just talking about this as our plane landed. I'm not really sure of my direction, but I want adventure. Actually, I don't want to follow in Mom's footsteps of marriage and family right away.' She gives me a side glance. "I want to explore the world and see if I can make it on my own."

That child never misses an opportunity.

"I always set an intention for my Camino," Sister Sophia says. "This trip is to guide those who choose back to the church. The church has lost so many people because it has lost its spirit. I want to share the spirit of the faith, not all the rules and regulations."

Sister Sophia and Emily seem to be on the same wavelength. I hadn't thought about the church's view of women. I know the rules. They're easy for me. I go to church because that's the expectation. The church is what binds our family together. But do I have 'spirit'?

Camille breaks into my thoughts. "I'm a widow and an empty nester. When Sister Sophia came to our church, I saw this as an opportunity to espouse my faith and lead people back to the Catholic church. This is my purpose. And I'm out of shape and hope this will fix that problem." Most everyone at the table smiles.

The introductions continue around the table then Peter motions to Gwen, the cook and housekeeper. She sets a huge bowl of salad on the table, and I can smell the fresh vegetables as I fill my plate. My first bite tells me they are freshly picked. The flavor explodes in my mouth. Peter tells us about the community garden at the edge of town where they grow their produce. I love my little garden back home, but sandy Florida soil and bugs always seem to have a way of winning.

The next course is a paella. This is what I smelled cooking in the kitchen as I set the table. Peter comes out of the kitchen carrying a pan that has to be at least two feet in diameter and heaped with yellow rice and vegetables. The smell of saffron and garlic spice the air.

If that isn't enough, after we polish off the last of the crispy rice on the bottom of the pan which Peter tells us is called *socarrat. I just call it delicious.* He brings in a bountiful tray of fruits and cheeses for dessert. He says the cheese is made right here in the Pyrenees. The soft texture and mild flavor are lovely with the fruit and the dessert wine.

"You know wine is a recognized food group in France," Peter tells us with a wink. I love the idea of a food pyramid with wine at the top.

After dinner, we head to our rooms to sleep. It's going to be an early start and Peter promises that we will be woken by angels in time for breakfast.

The next morning, beautiful music floats down the hall. It's a chant of women's voices. Rising I walk down the hall to wash up for breakfast. The bathroom is occupied. I go sit on my bed while the other ladies get up. I sneak a peek at the potions Jackie is taking out of her pack when a male voice calls "Next." I take my turn in the bathroom. He was faster than the boys at home.

At breakfast, Peter gives us the weather report. It's about ten degrees Celsius and foggy this morning, but by after-noon it will be sunny and clear getting up to twenty-one degrees. I grab my phone out of my fanny pack and do a quick conversion. It's about fifty degrees now and will warm up to about 70 degrees. I tuck the scarf around my neck, into the collar of my jacket in defense of the cold. We put on our boots, shoulder our packs, and head out the door. The fog curls its way up and down the street, making landmarks come in and out of focus, like my brain.

There is a brass scallop shell embedded in the road, so we stop and take pictures of the shell alongside our boots. Proof that we are on our way. The next stop is at the church of the Notre Dame of the Assumption of the Virgin. I light a candle for my family and say a silent prayer. Sister Sophia sits quietly in a pew as we each take our time in spiritual preparation. She then stands and gathers us in front of the altar where we say a prayer before heading up the mountain.

This is said to be the toughest part of the Camino. I'm hardly out of town when I already can't seem to catch my breath. And I thought I was ready. This is brutal.

Sister Sophia walks up next to me, "Slow down. Santiago will still be there when you arrive. It's been there waiting for you for fifteen hundred years, a few more minutes won't matter."

Hannah, who seems to be doing just fine and asks if she could go ahead with Sister. I nod, unable to spare my breath. Emily is in front of me, and I've been trying to match her pace. I watched her disappear around the next curve. Taking the opportunity to stop and look around.

The morning fog has disappeared, and the sky is a bright blue. Red poppy blossoms are just starting to peek out at the edge of the field, believing that summer is finally coming. A horse is eating its breakfast on the other side of the fence, it stops and looks up at me asking for a treat. I shrug shaking my head 'no' and it goes back to eating grass.

The red roof of a barn is just visible beyond the next rise. A green sea of hay is waving in the wind, it makes me think of the line 'amber waves of grain.' It's not so different here than in parts of the US.

"Same, same, but different," Sister Sophia said on the van ride yesterday when Emily asked her about the terrain. Mountains are mountains. But there's something about this ancient route, surrounded by legend and mystery that is amplified by these heights. In my next deep breath, I become aware of the fragrance of the earth. Such a clean and vital smell. Even the sheep smell clean, as they graze their way up the far slope. *I'm not in Florida anymore.* My silly quip puts a smile on my face.

I feel for the scarf around my neck and loosen it as the sun warms my back. The fine wool and the beautiful colors glow in the sun. I think about Mary walking up this mountain and all the way to Santiago. It seems so far away. I look at the scarf and pray. *Please give me energy and keep Hannah safe. So, we can make it to Santiago to dance in front of the cathedral.*

CHAPTER 4

ORRISON

I start walking once again, leaning into the mountain, watching every foot placement on the uneven track. The snow must do a number on these roads in the winter.

"Helen, watch out," Camille calls from behind me. At the sound of barking, I look up. There's a dog herding thousands of sheep straight towards me. I jump off the road and flatten myself against a fence. Camille joins me and we wait for the herd to go by.

"Have you ever seen anything like that?"

"We have cattle, not sheep, and they're certainly not herded down the middle of the road," she says.

We step back onto the path and can't avoid the sheep manure that squishes under our boots. Now I know why they ask pilgrims to leave their boots at the front door. The earthy odor is pungent in the air. It touches something inside of me that is primordial. I can imagine a good rainstorm coming along and washing it into the fields to nourish the ripening grain.

As Camille and I round the next bend, Sister Sophia is waving at us from the porch of the gite. What a relief. We made it, celebrating with a high-five. The first day accomplished. Sister Sophia gives us our room number and a token for our five-minute shower. This is going to be interesting. Hannah has never taken a five-minute shower in her life.

I make my way up to the room, while Camille makes a bathroom stop. There are ten bunk beds. I put my backpack on the floor and claim a bottom bunk by rolling out my sleeping bag. I glance up at the sound of a male voice speaking French. He and his companion are deciding which bunks they will sleep on in our room. Welcome to the Camino. I knew we would be sharing sleeping space with other pilgrims, but I had not thought it would be men. I assumed we would be separated by gender.

Jackie comes in, looks at the two men from France, then looks at me and winks. This woman is going to be the death of me. I grab my toiletries, clean clothes, and head off to my five-minute shower. At least the showers are separated by gender.

There is a foyer to my shower where I hang my dry clothes on a hook over my fanny pack, get undressed, and put my dirty clothes in my laundry bag. Sliding the token onto the slot on the wall a jet of lukewarm water hits me.

After the shower, I grab Hannah's dirty clothes. Amazing. She actually managed to shower in five minutes. The water temperature must have kept her from dallying. I'll have to try this at home.

I head to the laundry sink, wash our clothes by hand, and hang them on the line to dry. Thank goodness I had insisted on 'old lady underwear' for Hannah. She had wanted to bring the frilly bikini ones that all the young girls are so crazy about, but I didn't think they would be practical or very modest.

I make my way into the dining room, which also serves as a gathering place. A woman standing at the bar turns and smiles. Introducing myself, she replies, saying her name is Aino. She orders a glass of wine in English with a strong accent that I just can't place. Definitely not Spanish, almost sounds Scandinavian. Smiling at the bartender I ask for the same.

Hannah joins us. "Mom, is it alright for me to have a glass of wine?"

"Yes, dear, you're eighteen and it's part of the culture."

We take our wine out to the patio perched on the side of the mountain overlooking the valley. The sun is casting long shadows on the fields, lighting up the sky in pinks and reds as it sinks behind the mountains.

"It's so beautiful," I exclaim.

"Where are you from in America?" Aino asks.

"We're from Florida. We don't have mountain views and sunsets like this."

"But you have Micky Mouse," she says.

"Micky Mouse, again. Is that all people think of when they hear the word Florida? We have beautiful beaches, reefs, and, of course, the Everglades."

"Oh, I did not mean to offend. I was making a joke."

"I'm sorry. I've heard that joke too many times already on this trip." My annoyance surprises me. This woman had done nothing wrong.

"Your daughter, she is lovely."

"Thank you," I say, starting again in a friendlier vein. "Do you have children?"

"No, I do not."

Emily and Camille walk up to us, their glasses of wine in hand. We make introductions all around.

"Sister Sophia is inside reserving a dinner table for us and Jackie's just finishing her shower. You are welcome to join us," Camille says to Aino. "Did you start your Camino in St. Jean?"

"No, I started in Paris. I would be pleased to join you, then I can practice my English."

Paris, oh my. "Your English is perfect," I say, feeling a bit ashamed of my inability to speak other languages.

"Where are you from?" Camille asks.

"Finland," Aino says. "We do not get too many Americans visiting us, but we are required to learn English in school. Who is Sister Sophia?"

"She's our leader and from Spain. Part of her mission is to lead women on Pilgrimages and deepen our connection to the church. Right now, I think it's torturing women, a leftover from the Inquisition." I said with a smile. "My, she's strong. She took off right up that mountain. I'm beat and it is only our first day. Thirty-two more days to go. I don't know if I'll make it."

"Oh yes you will," Emily says. "Look at that view. It makes the slog uphill worth every step. It reminds me of home. We have wonderful mountains in Seattle. I go to the top to get lost in the view."

"That's why you were the first to arrive. You're used to walking in the mountains," Camille adds.

"Yes, but I'm not looking forward to the flat Meseta. I'm afraid it'll be boring."

Camille shakes her head. "I'm looking forward to the Meseta, flat is for me. After a day like today, I'm ready to be done with the mountains. Tomorrow, we must walk seventeen kilometers, that's ten miles over the mountains. Though, if it's anything like today I might as well give up now."

"Camille let's stick together tomorrow," I suggest. "We walk about the same pace. We can let the mountain goats go ahead and stake out a bed and food for us."

"Goats! She called us goats. I guess that means we are the 'greatest of all time'." Emily laughs and hooks arms with Aino and Hannah. They make their way into dinner with Camille and me trailing behind.

Dawn breaks early in the mountains. We pick up our lunch of *bocadillos* and shoulder our packs for the long trek over the Pyrenees, each of us finding our rhythm. The road takes us up to a cattle gate, the yellow arrows pointing us up a rocky, dirt trail toward the summit.

Yesterday in the van Sister explained that the purpose of the yellow arrows is to keep pilgrims from getting lost. In case we get separated all we have to do is keep following the arrows and we will meet up. Sister told us the story of Don Elías Valiña Sampedro, who was a parish priest. In 1984, he made it his mission to trail along the Camino. He drove his car across northern Spain with gallons of yellow highway paint, marking the trail with arrows. He also recruited villagers to maintain the trails in their region.

Sister went on to say that if we haven't seen an arrow in fifteen minutes, we are to stop and go back to the previous arrow to make sure we are on track. I can't even imagine getting off the trail and having to backtrack. That sounds like absolute misery.

Jackie and Hannah are ahead of me, laughing with the men from France. Camille is trudging along behind them. I must talk to Hannah about foreign men.

Sister Sophia and Emily are not even in sight. Aino must be with them. I'm hoping that the peak I see just ahead is the top and we can start the descent. I put my head down and lean into the steep slope. I'm not going to let this mountain defeat me.

Bringing up the rear, again, I come upon Camille who is sitting on a rock with her boots off.

"My heels, they hurt so badly. I really did break these boots in. It must be the incline getting to me."

Grateful for the chance to stop and breathe, I take a look at her feet. The skin is raw, and blisters are forming. I get my first aid kit from my pack. "I have some cleanser, moleskin, and Vaseline. Let me fix them up for you. Do you have a dry pair of socks? These are wringing wet."

"Yes, they're here in my pack somewhere." She grimaces as I apply cleanser and the bandages. "I believe you have done this before."

"Yes, I was a nurse before I got married, but that was many years ago. I sometimes think I might like to go back to it. I really miss it."

"A nurse. No wonder. That must have been so fulfilling. I worked as a secretary at Hallmark. I had to get a job after

John died. Being a farm girl didn't qualify me for much else."

"I'm so sorry to hear of your loss."

"It was a long time ago. A sudden heart attack and he was only forty-two. I had to go back to work to make ends meet and take care of the children. I'm so grateful for the church. It became my mainstay. But enough about me. How did you like being a nurse?"

"I loved my job."

"So why did you quit?" Camille seems genuinely interested.

"Well, I married young and got pregnant. I couldn't continue working and raise a family at the same time. Besides Ken makes a good living as a surgeon and there was no need."

"Ah, so you married a doctor," Camille says as if it's obvious that women only become nurses to marry doctors.

"Yes, but things aren't so good right now." *Where did that come from?*

"I would have never guessed it the way you talk about him," she says, gently touching my forearm. "Is he mean to you?"

"Oh no. Not at all. He's a really kind man. We've been together since college. He's all I know. He's very content and has always been. I don't know why I'm so restless. Probably just getting close to being an empty nester. Hannah is off the college this fall, the twins are right behind her, and Ken has his work." *Now why did I just tell her all that? It must be the altitude.*

"You have a lot to think about. I too, feel restless, with the children on their own. I wonder what's next for me."

We both sit silently for a minute, lost in our thoughts. A bird soars overhead and I momentarily envy its wings.

"Ken's been a good husband," I say, trying to make up for my transgression. "But something is missing. I just don't have... those feelings towards him. When I look back, I don't think I ever had those feelings, even on the honeymoon. It was just something I was supposed to do. I was brought up to find a husband, get married, and have children."

Oh, you hypocrite, Helen. You've spent hours lecturing Hannah about the importance of finding a husband and having children and now here you are second guessing yourself.

I decide to call and check in with Ken when I get to Roncesvalles.

"I don't mean to pry." Camille switches out her socks for a pair of fresh ones and puts on her shoes.

"Not at all. I don't know what made me open up so easily. Maybe this is part of the Way. Hopefully, we'll both get some answers."

"Well, we better get going, we have a long way to go to Roncesvalles."

"I am not sure how you're going to keep walking with those blisters."

Camille stands up and takes a few steps to test her ability. "In First Peter verse four, it says: 'Therefore, since Christ suffered in his body, arm yourselves also with the same attitude, because whoever suffers in the body is done with sin. As a result, they do not live the rest of their earthly lives for evil human desires, but rather for the will of God.' I live to the word and the will of God. He set me out on this journey and there must be a reason for these blisters. Maybe they happened to remind you of being a nurse," she says, smiling.

"Well, I hate to think that you are suffering to help me find direction. You know your bible."

"It is my guide and my strength."

I admire her faith and determination as we make our way around the next bend.

"Hola," Sister's voice calls out to us. She is standing by a food truck. A food truck way up here in the middle of nowhere. A hot coffee would be just the thing. On the side of the truck is a whiteboard with a list of the countries that had been served that day. Finland is on the list. Aino must have already been through. I wonder if we'll meet up again.

We order coffee and I get a pastry to go with it. Just as we grab a seat at the one available table, Sister Sophia comes over to check in to make sure we are all right. Camille tells her about her blistered heels. I offer to stick with Camille and be her buddy. Sister, smiling, guesses that Emily is probably in Roncesvalles by now. She lets me know Hannah is ahead with Jackie in the company of the young men from France. We all laugh.

"Sister, I'm wondering how safe the Camino is for young girls?" I ask.

"The Camino's very safe. Pilgrims look after each other and the National Guard looks after all of us. The Camino doesn't need any bad press. But like everywhere, a person must stay alert and make good choices. Sometimes wine clouds people's judgment. But Hannah looks like she has a good head on her shoulders."

"Yes, she does, but I don't know anything about those young men hanging around her," I say.

"Don't worry, Jackie and Emily will keep an eye on her. But I know it must be hard seeing her grow up and want to go on her own, especially when we know that the world is not always kind to young women." Something about Sister Sophia's voice is very calming.

"Yes, that's what I worry about, but I know I can't keep her in a cage. She'll have to learn to fend for herself. I just don't want the lessons to destroy her life."

Sister Sophia sets down her coffee cup and looks at me. "Did you have to face hard lessons growing up?"

"Yes, I had an incident in nursing school with an

overzealous medical student, but that was a long time ago. I got through it unscathed. But with Hannah, we've kind of sheltered her. We've tried to teach her right from wrong, but I don't think she has ever been really challenged."

Sister Sophia nods. "I'm glad she is with you on this pilgrimage. It will challenge you both in unexpected ways. But as far as her being in physical danger, not to worry."

"Yes," Camille says. "It's hard to watch them grow beyond our control. I must rely on my faith in God to watch over my children and protect them now that they're out on their own. But they will always be my little ones. I believe Emily will keep Hannah on the straight and narrow, but I'm not so sure about Jackie." She bends down and adjusts one of her shoes. "How much further is it, Sister? My feet are so sore."

"Not much longer now, then we start back down," Sister Sophia tells us. "Going down is harder than going up."

Camille shakes her head. "Well, I'm already hurting so that's not too inspiring."

Sister laughs, tucking that errant curl back under her veil. "I suppose not. It does get easier. Trust me. But we can sit for a few more minutes and rest."

I'm grateful for the hot coffee and the reprieve. Sitting feels so good but I'm not sure I'll be able to get back up. "What makes you do this again and again?" I ask her.

"So far it has been hard walking, lots of snoring, a five-minute shower, and it's cold here in the mountains."

Sister Sophia doesn't hesitate with her answer. "I've been called. The Way has been a source of strength and absolution for the faithful for millennia. The Catholic religion has lost many followers, and some of those who remain are stuck in the dogma of tradition. As a woman in the church, this is one of the few roles I'm allowed to take. The Way has worked its magic in my life, reaffirming my direction and giving me purpose. I hope that for all of those who choose to walk the Way."

"That's why I'm here," Camille says, now removing her shoes. "I, too, want to bring people back to the true religion. Our family values have suffered since people have left the church. The church has become too lax. There is a purpose for our laws, traditions, and roles. We must abide by them. This is how Jesus wants it to be."

Sister Sophia turns and addresses me. "You said your purpose was to make memories with your daughter. Is there anything else that may be important?" She pushes me to reflect deeper.

"Yes, actually. Today I had to dust off some of my nursing skills and it felt good. I'm wondering if I need to go back to my profession. That means going back to school and renewing my license. I may be too old. It's probably a silly dream. I really don't need to work. Ken has provided well for us. But it does feel good to use my skills to help others. Maybe that's what's missing. I just don't know."

Sister Sophia takes the last sip of her coffee before she answers, "You have close to five hundred miles to go before you need to make any decisions. Allow the path to clear your mind, and rest before you make a decision you may regret." She adjusts the length of her hiking poles and stands up. Once her pack is shouldered, she prompts us with a, "Let's talk as we walk."

I put my pack back on, feeling its weight bearing down on me. How on earth is Jackie carrying make-up too?

Once Camille gets her shoes back on, we step out from behind the food truck. A fresh breeze catches me by surprise, and I adjust the scarf on my neck. We continue our way up the mountain.

Clear my mind? Easier said than done. Many of my duties as a mother are coming to an end. My role as a wife? I am not going to have any more children, so what's the purpose of our relationship? Ken would think I'm being silly, but he has a purpose, a reason to get up in the morning. I guess grand-children could be a purpose, but Hannah's not interested. I wouldn't want to put that on her either. It's hard work raising children. Do I even have any skills? Could I even make it in today's nursing with all the technology? Am I obsolete?

A sudden slip on the rocks puts me on my butt and jolts me into the present.

"Are you alright?" Camille offers me her hand.

Sister Sophia suggests I check myself out before taking Camille's hand to help me stand up.

I check for damages and dust myself off. "Yes, I'm fine, just hurt my pride. I'm glad I fell on the most padded part of my body." I laugh and reach for her hand. "I'll have to be more careful and pay attention to each step. This is not easy."

"No really," Camille says. "If you're hurt it's the least I can do to go on ahead and get help. I'm sure Sister would stay here with you."

"Honestly, I'm fine," I shake my legs and wiggle my hips. "Everything seems to be working."

"Extend your poles a bit. They will give you more purchase on the downslope," Sister suggests. "Don't try to go too fast. The others will stake out our bunks at the Monastery."

The thought of a waiting bed propels me forward.

CHAPTER 5

RONCESVALLES TO PAMPLONA

"Hey!"

Jackie is calling to us as Sister, Camille and I walk out of the monastery into the street. In front of us, a bar with tables full of pilgrims encroaches upon the roadway. Jackie waves from a table in the middle of the crowd, where Emily, Hannah, and Aino are also sitting. Frosty beer mugs in several states of emptiness sit in front of them.

"Take a load off," Hannah says, laughing at her own joke. "How was your walk down the mountain?"

"Sister Sophia was right, it's harder going down than up," I tell her. "My poor toes are so sore. And my bottom – I could sure use a beer." Joining them at the table, I turn to my walking companions. "Sister, Camille, may I get you something?"

"Yes, please. A glass of red wine. You know we're getting into wine country. I believe that's my real reason for walking the Way so regularly," Sister says with a wink. "Spain produces the best wine in the world."

Camille grabs a seat next to Hannah. "I could use a beer, too, if you don't mind. I just don't think I can stand up again."

"Why's your bottom sore, Mom?" Hannah asks.

"I had a little slip, but I'm fine," I leave to make my way to the bar. *Don't let them see you sweat.*

"Are you alright?" Aino asks Camille.

"No, my heels are on fire. Helen bandaged them for me, and I put on dry socks, but they hurt so badly."

"It took me several weeks to get the right sock combination and toughen my heels," Aino tells her. "I will share some bandages with you after your shower."

Camille shakes her head. "I didn't even think of bringing bandages."

"I'm a doctor," Aino says. "I always have bandages."

"A doctor?" I say, returning to the table with a waiter to take our order.

"Yes, I work for, *Médecins sans Frontières.*"

"Doctors without Borders. I've heard of the wonderful work they do. I've even thought about becoming a volunteer."

"Are you a doctor?" Aino asks me.

"No, as a student nurse, I studied labor and delivery. I dreamed about working with young mothers in foreign countries."

"We could use good nurses. War seems to beget babies.

I guess people must find pleasure amongst all the pain." Aino takes a sip of her beer. "I had to take a break; I have been working in Afghanistan. The suffering is overwhelming. I don't know if I can go back. That is why I walk the Camino, to help me reflect on the next phase of my life."

Sister Sophia stands and pushes an errant curl back under her veil. "Well, drink up ladies. We must get ready for dinner and then the pilgrims' mass."

We make our way back to the albergue to get ready for the evening. Doctors Without Borders. I must learn more. Maybe this is what I have been looking for. I haven't used my French since college, but I wonder if I could get my language and nursing skills to a point where I could be useful.

As I pull myself up the stairs with the handrail to our assigned floor, I'm amazed at the size of the structure. According to the guidebook, it was originally built in the 1200's to house pilgrims and can hold almost two hundred of us at one time. The interior has definitely been updated a few times since then. I hear there are hot showers and comfortable mattresses. I'm too tired to care about anything else.

I wake to the rustling of pilgrims loading up their packs. As I reach to pick up my phone, I feel a hot poker sear its way up my rib cage. Grabbing the phone, I flop back down and pray for relief. What the heck?

The few deep breaths I take only exasperate the pain. Breathing- oh yeah - I've worked my lungs harder the past two days than I have in years. Here I was worried about my feet and legs and it's my ribcage that's taking the abuse.

The clock on my phone tells me it's 6 a.m. No wonder people are getting ready to walk. *God, please help me get out of bed.*

I texted Ken last night to let him know we had made it over the mountains, and I asked about the boys. Given the six-hour time difference, he hadn't seen it until this morning. Now I read, *Congratulations! boys r fine.* Sounds like they are surviving without me.

Camille motions to me from where she's sitting on her bed. "Helen, can you help me with my heels?"

"Can you help me stand up?" I say laughing, as I gingerly swing my legs over the edge of the bed and push myself up into a sitting position. "But yes, no problem. I have to use the ladies' room first." I slowly get to my feet. and my legs protest my command to walk forward. Hunched over like a one-hundred-and-ten-year-old woman, I make my way to the bathroom.

I sit down on the hard toilet seat, and my body launches

me straight up in pain. I forgot that I took that spill yesterday. As slowly as my sore legs allow, and holding onto the stall wall for support, I ease myself into the appropriate position for my morning ablutions.

I hear Sister cheerfully greet Hannah as they enter the bathroom.

How can they sound so chipper?

I'll just wait here until they're done. Then I can move. I don't want Hannah to see me in this state.

I finish and slowly stand up, using the walls for support. Thank God for small stalls. I stretch my muscles and check for permanent damage. Everything works. It just hurts.

I open the stall door and make sure the coast is clear then make my way back to the sleeping area. The walk down the long hall starts to oil the old joints a bit.

Camille is sitting on her bunk, patiently waiting for me to dress her heels. They look a bit like raw hamburger. She is in worse shape than I am and I'm not sure how she is going to walk, but she is determined.

Showered, laundered, fed, and well rested, we hobble our way to Zubiri, then we push on to Pamplona the next afternoon. There, Camille and I catch up with the rest of the group at the Albergue Plaza Catedral. Sister Sophia has reserved us a room with our own private bathroom. What a relief not to have to be in a crowded albergue.

Hannah walks over to Camille and me. "Let's go, we're meeting the French men at Café Iruña. That's where Hemingway used to hang out." Hannah had brushed her hair until it shone, then braided it and tucked the braid through the opening in the back of her cap.

"I'm going to stay here and rest. You all go have fun," Camille says.

"I have to go to the cathedral and make arrangements for our tour and service tomorrow," Sister says. "I'll see you all in the later."

The rest of us make our way to Café Iruña. We find an empty table close to the square. Emily sits down next to me and hands me a menu. "How are you holding up?"

"I am doing a bit better, but I'm hungry, must be all the walking. I would never eat like this at home," I say, looking down at my tummy. I had hoped walking would solve this problem, but the way I'm eating may negate all the exercise. "I'm worried about Camille. I am so thankful that tomorrow is a rest day before we head up to Alto de Perdón."

"So am I," Emily says. "I've been pushing myself a bit too hard. I just can't seem to slow down. My shins are sore."

"You, sore? I would've never guessed. Slowing down would be a good idea then. I know it's important to walk at your own pace, but maybe your pace is slower than you think."

Emily laughs. "You may be correct. One of the reasons

I came on this trip was to slow down. Old habits die hard."

"Is it what you thought it would be?" I ask.

"It's harder than I thought it would be. Carrying a pack every day is different from going out for my morning run. My life has become so fast-paced that I've lost perspective. It's 'get up, run, shower, breakfast, work, home, dinner, bed, and do it all over again'," Emily says. "I have been working so hard to climb the ladder and I don't know why,"

"Exactly what do you do in the tech field?" I ask.

"I'm an expert in designing software and manage a team working on new applications. It is hard to stay ahead of the younger native users. I'm getting old, but I don't want to become irrelevant," said Emily.

"Old, irrelevant. If you don't mind me asking, how old are you?" *Jeez, if she is afraid of becoming irrelevant, where does that leave me?*

The waiter arrives at our table and asks what we'd all like to order.

Emily requests a *vino tinto,* then says, "I just turned forty. This trip is a birthday gift to myself."

"I'll have the same," I tell the waiter then turn my attention back to Emily. "Doesn't your experience count?"

"In this field, things change so fast, it's not about experience. It's about being on the cutting edge. You blink and you get behind. I'm taking a risk with this leave of absence. Thank goodness my supervisor is Catholic, and she understands. She supported my decision. I just hope I have a job when I get back and some youngster hasn't wormed their way past me. But I felt it was worth the risk for my sanity."

"Yes, you're right. Sanity is so important. Somehow we lose it in the ordinary routine of our lives." I gesture across the table, "What do you think about those young French men?"

"They're a bit flirtatious but harmless. And Hannah is not doing anything to encourage them. She seems to have a good head on her shoulders. But if would make you feel better, I'm happy to keep an eye out."

"Oh Emily, I appreciate that. I don't want to hold her back, but I also don't want her to get hurt. Life can be harsh."

The waiter places our glasses of wine in front of us. I take a sip, smile at him and nod.

"I know." Tears well up in Emily's eyes, but she turns her head and shakes it off. I don't want to pry.

Jackie yells to us from where she is seated with the French men. "Hey girls, come join the party."

Emily and I smile at each other, pick up our wine glasses, and move closer to the group. Maybe I can use my time on the Camino to improve my French and keep an eye on these young men.

The next morning, we head to the cathedral for a tour and the pilgrims' mass. Walking around without the backpack is such a relief. Camille seems a little better too. She soaked her feet in Epsom salts and said it really helped.

After the service, we go back to the albergue to rest, then to the convent for a dinner Sister has arranged with the local order. One of the older nuns tells a story about a family on the outskirts of town who lost a child to a farming accident. The entire community came together to help this family.

"The sisters are committed to their mission of taking care of pilgrims and their community," Sister Sophia says, translating as the older nun speaks.

The compassion on the nun's face is so inspiring. She makes me think about our church community. We have our charitable events, but I don't seem to feel the same connection to my neighbors as she is describing. I don't really know what is going on behind their closed doors down the street. No one even comes over to borrow a cup of sugar. We're all so busy at jobs or taking care of our children that we rarely connect. It doesn't feel like much of a community.

On the other hand, maybe I haven't made time to be part of my community. But no one else seems to do so either. We all just sit in our own little universes, watching

TV or playing on the computer. If someone on our block lost their child, would we rally around? Or would we just stay away because we don't know what to do?

This has given me a great deal to think about.

CHAPTER 6

ALTO DE PERDÓN TO PUENTE LA REINA

The next morning, we grab a quick cup of coffee and a roll, shoulder our packs, and head to Alto de Perdón, the Mount of Forgiveness. We make our way along the city sidewalks which morph onto a gravel farming track that makes its way straight up the mountain. I lean into the mountain with Hannah cheering me on. Emily joins us, making good on her commitment to walk slower. Sister, Camille, and Jackie are bringing up the rear. Today we will gain three hundred fifty meters of elevation in about fourteen kilometers. Then it will be all downhill from there.

I dread this downhill. I have heard other pilgrims say it's tougher than the one into Roncesvalles because of the loose rock. I stop for a minute to catch my breath and Emily just keeps forging ahead. So much for breaking habits. She quickly increases the distance between us. I wonder if I will ever get into that kind of shape.

Hannah is steady beside me and doesn't seem the worse for wear. I smile at her but don't say anything as I only have enough breath for walking. She smiles back and starts humming that song *'Ultreia,'* the one Sister taught us in Pamplona. I join Hannah in the chorus.

"Ultreia et Suseia, onward and upward".

Somehow the singing eases my breathing, and up we go with the crunching sound of the gravel under our feet adding percussion to our song.

I spy a bench under a tree and guide Hannah towards it. I sit take off my boots and stretch my feet. I take a pack of almonds from my pack and hand her some. How are you?".

"Oh, Mom, it's so awesome." Her face is lit up with joy.

"I see you're making friends quite easily. Tell me about the young men from France." I unwind the scarf from around my neck and hear a voice inside my head say, "Listen."

"Oh Mom, it's nothing like that. They're nice and have been complete gentlemen. It's really cool to learn about their culture. André is studying international business and Jean studies chemistry. He hopes to go to medical school. Besides, I've seen what marriage to a doctor is like and I'm not ready for that. I want to pursue my dreams. I want to travel."

"What do you mean by 'seeing what our marriage is like'?"

This child has no clue what she is talking about. She is baiting me again and I'm not going to take it. Turning the tables so she doesn't have to make any future plans. We have a solid marriage, and we never fight, at least not in front of the children.

I meet her gaze and wait for an answer.

"Well, Mom, it's not bad...but Dad is hardly ever home, and you are caught up in our lives, taking care of the house and doing your volunteer work for the church. I don't know who you are separate from Dad. But, I want to know who I am."

Tears spring to my eyes and I turn away, so she won't notice. Does she really just see me as an extension of Ken and not as my own person? I was taught to be a good wife and mother. Isn't that enough?

"Be careful judging. You've had an idyllic childhood because you have parents who care."

"Yes, you've always been there for me. But I see a larger world. The world was different when you got married. You did what you were supposed to do. I don't want to get caught in that trap." Hannah pulls off her hat and brings her braid over her shoulder.

Oh, this child. Patience...

"I am not trapped." The words come out a bit harsher than I intend. "I do the things that I know are important. Raising you all and taking care of your father is important."

"But is it your passion? I just don't see the passion in

your life. You just smile and go through your daily duties," She looks at me with intensity and starts twirling the end of her braid – always the clue that she is stepping out on a limb and uncomfortable.

"Raising you and your brothers was more than a duty. I love all of you and wanted you more than anything on earth. I call that passion. I want to watch you grow into your lives. Have you gotten more clarity on what you want to do besides just travel?"

"Well, remember those travel shows we watch at home? I would love to be a host. I know my language skills aren't very strong, but I do love history and I think it would be great to be an archeologist like Nancy White or an anthropologist like Margaret Mead."

I glance around and realize the others have moved on way ahead of us. Just as well. I want this private time with my daughter.

"An archeologist or anthropologist? You know that means college, not just going off-traveling, right? You have been accepted at Hillsborough Community College."

Hannah pulls her braid back through the hole in her cap and resettles it on her head. "Well, yeah. I'm just starting to put it together. It could work a couple of ways. I could hire myself out as a laborer at a dig and learn by doing, or I could go to college first. I have a little more exploring to do."

"Yes, I know you want to find your passion, to find your-self. Passion is not all there is in life. Safety and commitment are important too. You are so gifted. I believe college will help you hone your gifts and give you direction. A young woman needs to have a secure job to fall back on. Ken has provided well for all of us, and I got to be with you and the twins. If it was not for his job, we would not be here now."

"Dad is passionate about his job. He's excited to go to the hospital and treat his patients. I don't see that same fire in you."

"Just because I'm not 'passionate' doesn't mean I am not content."

"But I don't want your kind of content. I want adventure."

I smile at her youthful enthusiasm. "Well then, pick up your pack, and let's go find some adventure. I didn't bring you all the way to Spain to sit under a tree."

Laughing, Hannah gets up and shoulders her pack.

I grab mine and we continue our way up the mountain. I find Emily sitting at a fountain, waiting for us. The steep narrow rock path is right behind her. This will be our final climb to the top. Intimidated, I stop and sit beside her but Hannah heads on up the mountain.

"I did it again," Emily says.

"Yep, old habits are hard to break. I envy your ability. I hope to be able to keep up with you by the time we reach O'Cebreiro."

"I want to slow down, and you want to speed up. Neither of us are satisfied." She stands and motions for me to follow. "Come on, race you to the top!"

Somehow, I find the strength to laugh and join her. We launch ourselves up the path. As we top the ridge, the metal sculpture depicting pilgrims comes into view. Windmills are stretched out along the mountaintop, humming and generating electricity for the city below. Hannah and Jackie are already getting their pictures taken in front of the metal pilgrims with the French men. I walk over to the granite memorial which commemorates those who have lost their lives fighting for social justice in 1936 and 1937. The inscription reads:

> This is a tribute to the victims and their families who were killed for fighting for their ideals of social justice and democracy. In Navarra, there wasn't a front during the war, and these people were killed without a trial, deprived of their homes by force, and buried in mass graves in this land, all of them forgotten and silenced for 81 years by the institutions.

Aino is sitting on one of the granite slabs at the foot of the pillar. I ask if I can join her. She smiles and indicates a place next to her.

"You know the metal sculpture over there is the most famous. But this memorial speaks to me," she says. "It honors all those who have lost their lives fighting for their ideals. I have never lived in oppression where I needed to fight for my ideals. My country accepts my sexual preference. I have never been treated as different."

"Are you gay?"

"A lesbian, yes," Aino says.

"In my country, it is just starting to be accepted, but there is still a stigma. In Finland is it well accepted?"

"Yes, I had a long-term partner, but she died of breast cancer two years ago." Her bottom lip quivers. "That is when I started with Médecins sans Frontières. I knew I would not make the same money, but I did not care. I had to get away and see if there was someone I could help."

I can see the pain etched on her face. I've never lost anyone that I have loved like that so I just can't even imagine. I rummage in my fanny pack for some tissue. Splitting it, I give her half and keep half. We sit quietly together, blotting our tears.

Camille and Sister arrive and Hannah calls to me to join her. I turn to Aino, hug her, then head over for a group picture. I look at the sculpture. It depicts all the ways in which a pilgrim can make this journey. There are pilgrims walking and on horseback. One pilgrim is leading a donkey carrying his pack. I want a donkey to carry my pack down this mountain and all the way to Santiago.

Hannah is standing next to a cutout of a pilgrim striding into the future. It won't be long before she walks out of my life and into her own. I wonder what is ahead on her path. I don't want her to get hurt or make mistakes.

We walk over to a plaque in front of the sculpture and Sister translates for us. "Where the path of the wind crosses that of the stars."

I wonder where the wind will take me. Is contentment enough? I'm not sure I was ever passionate about anything. Nursing was to be a good solid career. I knew I could always get a job. Ken is a good solid husband. I have three great kids. What more should I ask for? God has been very good to me, better than I deserve.

Sister, Hannah, Jackie, and the French men lead the way off the mountain. The path down the mountain quickly becomes treacherous. My toes are banging up against the front of my boots and the loose shale is slipping beneath my feet. One false move and my Camino may be over. I've heard of people getting injured and not being able to complete their Caminos. That would be so devastating.

Aino is in front, zigzagging down the mountain. I start to zig-zag my way down, leaning on my poles for support. I motion to Camille to follow my lead. It feels much safer, and my toes are not taking such a beating. Emily hangs back with us for moral support. It will be a relief when we finally get to the bottom and our albergue for the night. To motivate us, Sister Sophia tells us about Estella, the next large city. She says it is one of her favorites and that we would be there for the festival. We should arrive in two days. *If I can survive the next two days.*

CHAPTER 7

ESTELLA

As we walk into the town of Estella Camille is doing a little better. The bandages and nightly soaks have been helping. Sister has rented us an apartment for the night. She thinks it will be good to have our own space for a change. It even has a washer and dryer. Things that I took for granted at home have now become luxuries.

We settle in, get our showers, and do laundry. Things are starting to get lively as we walk into the town square. It is fiesta time. We find a table and order wine just as a parade comes through the town square. First, the jesters. At least that is what they look like to me, with their black and white checkered outfits, pointed hats, and shoes. The bells on their hats and shoes jiggle as they pass by our table. Next, a beautiful band of dancers with their colorful skirts swirling, as they spin their way down the street. Then the walking heads. Sister explains that these date back to the 1200s. They represent archetypes and historical figures. Some of the heads represent demons that cause temptation, and they are used to scare children from committing mischief. I could have used them for the twins!

Two ladies on a horse, riding back-to-back, pass by and my heart catches. One is totally white the other totally black. Sister tells us that these two ladies represent the side we show the world, the white face. And the side we keep hidden even from ourselves, the black face, she calls our shadow side. I'm not sure I'm that complex.

There is a small band followed by more dancers. Sister indicates we should get up and join in. I'd never really thought about nuns dancing, but here she is. She walks the Camino, she dances... and now I see more than one curl escaping from her veil.

My poor body. Dancing after walking all day? But Hannah grabs the ends of the scarf around my neck and pulls me to my feet. My spirit eclipses my tired mind and body as we twirl out into the square. Dancing with the scarf and laughing, we move with the fiesta around the square.

We arrive back at our table breathless as the waiter delivers our dinner. Perfect timing. This is such a magical place. This was the town where Mary had met the young woman who left the scarf behind. I wonder where the young woman is now and what she's doing. I hope her life is becoming all she wants it to be. I wonder if I, too, will get a direction. Passion! Dancing with abandon is passion and such fun. I can't even remember the last time I went dancing.

After dinner, we head back to our lodgings. I take my toiletries and go into the bathroom. Hannah is already at one of the sinks. I bump her over with my hip and she bumps back. Bumping, brushing, and giggling, we finish our night-time routine and head to bed. I was told by my girlfriends that once your child becomes an adult, you go from parent to friend. I believe we are making the transition.

Hannah was an easy child to raise. She seemed to always want to please, to do the right thing. Maybe it's because she is the oldest. The twins were such a handful when they were born, she became my little helper. Now, she did have her moments, but some of my friends had it much worse. I remember the time Hannah stayed out all night with her 'friends.' I was in a panic, imagining all the things that could happen to a young girl. When she got home we grounded her for a week. It never happened again.

After a good night's sleep, we shoulder our packs the next morning and head out the door. We have 21.5 kilometers to Los Arcos and who knows how many more to Santiago. I just have to keep putting one foot in front of the other. As we walk, memories of the fiesta last night make me smile. Hannah is so young with so much promise and I loved seeing her dancing around the square, first with her old mother and then when André grabbed her hand and Jean took mine and twirled us even faster. Breathless, back at the table, Hannah's face glowed as she talked to André.

Ken and I have been married for nineteen years. I'm not that old, just forty-two this year. Where did those feelings go, and were they ever there? I don't remember ever feeling giddy and glowing like Hannah. I hope she finds a wonderful man to make her happy and keep that glow. But I can't stand the thought of her marrying a French man and living in France. I would never get to see my grandchildren.

Aino shows up beside me. "Hello, Helen."

"Hello. I have been thinking about what you said about Doctors Without Borders. It sounds very tempting."

"Do you think your husband would let you go?"

Ken letting me go. He didn't seem to have a problem with our coming to Spain. In fact, he encouraged us to go. *Do I really need his permission?* I never before thought of our relationship in this way. We've always respected each other's decisions.

"I don't think he would miss me. He's married to his job," I say.

Aino looks at me quizzically. "I thought he was married to you."

"Oh, that is just an expression. It means that his job is more important to him than his marriage." I make a mental note to make sure I clarify my meanings.

"I am so sorry, Helen. It must be difficult for you."

"Oh, you misunderstand. Ken is kind and supportive. It's definitely not difficult. It's just how it is."

"Is that how it is?"

I stop walking and face her. "Aino, you are asking me some difficult questions and I don't think you have any right to pry."

"I am sorry. I just don't like to see you so sad," she says.

"Sad?"

"Yes, there is a light deep inside of you that is trying to burst forth."

"I'm afraid I'm too old for bursting forth." The thought of it makes me laugh.

"How old are you?"

"I just turned forty-two this year."

She smiles and says, "I am forty-four. We are just coming into our own as women. We should celebrate."

"Celebrate?"

"Yes, we will make a celebration when we get to Logroño. Now I must hurry forward. I have to make a stop and take care of some personal business, but I look forward to our celebration. *Buen Camino*." She smiles and hurries ahead.

"Buen Camino, Aino."

Coming into my own as a woman. What does that mean? Is it possible for me to leave Ken and go be a nurse in a foreign country, even if for a short time? I could go for a few months now that the children don't really need me anymore. Hannah will be in college and the twins are almost seventeen... Oh heck, what am I thinking?

I fiddle with the fringe on the scarf. A soft voice says, "Yes, you could."

"Hey, Helen," Jackie says as she catches up with me. "Was that Aino?"

"Yes, she has to go take care of some business, but she wants us to celebrate our 'coming into our own as women' when we reach Logroño. Have you ever heard of such a thing?"

"I want to be part of that celebration. I love being a woman!"

Jackie is like no one I've ever met before. How or why, she chose to walk the Camino is still a mystery to me, but she's nice enough and maybe she has insights I don't.

"What does that mean to you, being a woman?" I ask.

"A woman is like – well, in some ways like that scarf around your neck." She extends her hand; I unwrap the scarf from around my neck and hand it to her. "Each one of these threads represents a part of who we are. We are vibrant like the orange, bold like the red, the purple our spirit, the pink our soft sexy, all carefully cultivated and woven into a beautiful and strong whole.

Look at Camille, hardly a whimper and she just keeps on going despite the pain. That is one tough woman." She waves a hand in the air for emphasis. "Emily has such a deep kind soul despite being a tough corporate executive. Then there's sweet Hannah, who is so bright and fresh and has none of the hang-ups of having to be the 'little woman' to a man. She's so blessed to have been born in a time when women are allowed to be their authentic selves."

She places the scarf back around my neck. I examine the threads. "Each one of these threads also represents each one of us, stronger woven together."

She smiles and adjusts the scarf around my neck. "And you, Helen, the healer. We are just starting to tap your talents."

"And you?" I'm curious to know how she'll describe herself.

"Well, hell! I don't have to be what someone else wants me to be. I can live my dreams. I have the ability to make money and take care of myself. I don't have to depend on anyone, and I choose who I want to be with. I have a wonderful husband and I love being a wife. We're very sexually compatible. Even after twenty-five years, we're still like teenagers. This separation will just make things better when I get home. He's cool with me being here. I'm cool with him pursuing his dreams. It's what keeps us together. Mutual respect."

"I thought you were....well, open." I blurted out the words without thinking.

"Honey, whatever gave you that idea?"

"I saw you flirting with those young French men. I just assumed—"

"That's part of being a woman. Why can't I enjoy the company of young men? I decide what I will and will not do in a relationship, and I have no desire for a romp in the hay with those boys. Learning about their culture and the way they think is fun. I love their humor and their comfort in their own skin. They've been perfect gentlemen and I expect nothing less." Jackie raised her inquiring eyebrow at me.

"Maybe I should spend a little time with the French men. But it feels so strange to me."

"Isn't that why you're here? To get out of your comfort zone?"

"Well yes, I suppose so. I hadn't thought of it in quite that way."

"Then feel free to join us for a glass of wine. You always sit as far away from us as the table will allow."

I could feel myself blushing. "No, I don't. I just sit where there's room."

She patted my shoulder and winked. "Well then, we'll just make sure that there's room for you at our end of the table."

Sister Sophia joins us, looking as fresh as the cool spring morning. "Helen, Jackie, how are you doing today?"

"Very well, Sister. This has been an enlightening day," I tell her.

"Yes, it takes a few days to get quiet and get inside. Just wait until the Meseta."

Jackie asks what's so different about the Meseta.

"There's a theory that the Camino is broken into three sections. The first is the physical and by the time we reach Burgos, our bodies will be trail-hardened. The second section is the Meseta. It is the flat, uniform farmland that leads to inner reflection. It is spiritually the hardest part of the journey as you turn inside. You question yourself and get in touch with your shadow side. Remember the two women on the horse? We put forward our light face and keep our dark side behind us, our shadow side. On the Meseta, we see our shadow and are not always comfortable with what we see. When we reach Leon and start back into the mountains, we begin to integrate our two sides and become whole."

Sister stops and takes a deep breath. Her eyes get a distant look in them, and her face becomes quite still. "When I walked the Camino for the first time, I was struggling with my future. I didn't know what I was called to do. My family was encouraging me to meet a nice young, rich man and get married. I did not want for beaus, and I had the looks and the money to go with it. You see,

I was born into a rich family. My older brother was going to inherit, and I was to be given a dowry." She smiles, remembering. "My parents paraded so many eligible bachelors in front of me. I learned to be quite the coquette. But there was a part of me that knew I was just playing a game."

"But isn't that what women are taught to do, to make themselves attractive to men?" I ask. "My mother taught me never to appear smarter than a man or it would scare them off. Such silliness now that I look back."

Sister's face flushes as she adjusts her veil and checks for errant locks. "But I had no interest in men. I didn't want to marry. I loved the Lord, and this is what made my heart sing. To appease my family, I went to college and was given a job in the family business, but my heart was not in it. My parents suggested I walk the Camino to review my life choices and to make a decision. They said I should walk on my own means and not in the comfort of the family fortune. I quickly agreed and found the support of a local convent who sponsored my pilgrimage. I stayed in *donativo* and *parochial* alburgues, providing service as I walked across Spain. When I returned home, I was able to tell my parents that I wanted to go into the sisterhood. They agreed and I have never looked back."

To leave home and all you know with no means, except the support of your faith. Could I do this? Is my faith strong enough?

"You are strong enough," said the quiet voice in my head.

"Thank you, Sister. I hope I can find my way. Aino said she saw a light inside of me just waiting to burst out. I don't know about that. I am content with my life."

But is contentment enough?

I glance over at Jackie. There's a tear slipping down her cheek, but she smiles at me. "I am here to make sense of the loss of my mother. She died of breast cancer two years ago. Three months ago, I had the *BRCA* gene test, and it was positive. I had my breasts removed. I just couldn't risk getting the disease. I miss her so much. I worry about my daughter. She refuses to get the test. She's only twenty-three and has no conception of her mortality or what breast cancer means. I can't force her."

"Oh, I am so sorry." I give her a tissue from my fanny pack.

Jackie takes a moment to dab her eyes and nose. "I carry some of my mother's ashes. I want to leave them at Cruz de Ferro. I want to release the horror I remember from her death. I want to hold on to who she was before the cancer. I hope it will help."

Tears start sliding down my face. I reach out and hug her. She smiles at me, steps back, adjusts the scarf around my neck, and winks.

CHAPTER 8

LOGROÑO

As we make our way to Logroño, we start talking about our women's celebration party. I plan on showing Aino that we are "bringing it."

Did I really just think that?

Bringing it? So not me! But who am I? Maybe Aino is right. Maybe there is a light inside that I have never acknowledged.

"Yes, there is," the soft voice says.

"So, we party tonight?" Hannah asks me as we walk. "I vote for wine. We are in the Rioja region where they make the best wines in the world, and I want to experience it."

"Hannah, experiencing it is one thing, but you have to learn to drink responsibly," I remind her.

"Like you do?" Hannah shoots me a sideways glance. "I see the empty wine bottles building up in the trash and I know it's not Dad. He would never do anything to jeopardize his patients."

"I enjoy a glass in the afternoon. Have you ever been neglected?"

I won't say this to her, but I have sometimes wondered the same. A nice glass of wine on a quiet afternoon makes the time go by. The children don't really need me to drive them around anymore. Hannah has her own car, and the twins use mine. It's not like when they were young, and I had to do everything for them. Ken only needs my meals. He comes home exhausted, eats, and goes to sleep. I'm not hurting anyone. Even if I drink two glasses, I can still get a good nutritious meal on the table.

"Well, no." Hannah is a bit more subdued.

"Then this is how to drink responsibly," I tell her then quicken my pace to catch up with Sister Sophia. "Where are we staying in Logroño, Sister?"

"We're staying at the convent connected with the Santiago Real Church. It's a lovely place. There will be a mass, and then a community dinner. The doors lock at ten pm, so it will have to be an early celebration," She's looking at me and Hannah like she might've overheard our conversation and is now wondering if she should intervene.

"Oh Sister, what a spoilsport you are," Hannah says, breaking the tension.

"You will have plenty of time for adventure and fun without having to stay out late." Sister tells her. "I remember being your age and the parties we would attend. But in Spain we have chaperones. A young lady does not allow herself to be alone with a man before marriage. I know this sounds old-fashioned, but there is some wisdom here. Sometimes our biological drives mixed with alcohol lead us to do things we would not normally do."

I shoot Hannah my 'Don't you dare' look so she doesn't say anything to embarrass me.

"No need to worry. I'm not going to be in anyone's little black book," Hannah says. "I know what you're saying though. I saw it happen to a girl in my school. She drank too much at a party and left with a guy, we all know, who only wanted one thing. We tried to talk sense into her, but she wouldn't listen. Unfortunately, she had to have an abortion, at least that's what the rumor mill said. I didn't know her well, so I really don't know what's true. I would never compromise myself that way."

"You say 'never'," I tell her. "But sometimes things get out of control and go too far. I've seen it happen too. The woman is always the one who ends up suffering, not the man. That's one reason your father and I have been so protective of you. We don't want you to make a mistake you would regret. We love you too much. That's why I always like to see you with one of the other women when the French men are around. You'll have plenty of opportunity to celebrate your woman-hood – and not just by being out partying late." As an after-thought, I hurriedly add, "And it's not just about men!"

"Me making a mistake? What about the guy? It takes two to make a baby. Why does the blame always fall on the woman's shoulders? Why can't I enjoy myself and not have to worry about getting pregnant or hurt or ..." Her eyes blazed with anger.

I put my arm around her. "No, honey, it is not fair. The woman seems to carry the blame even though it does take two. There are no easy answers. I'm really glad there's birth control now. It wasn't available when I was growing up."

She hugs me back. We look at each other and smile.

"Now, speaking of parties, I wonder how I'm going to connect with Aino. We haven't exchanged phone numbers. I don't want her to think that I've forgotten our deal."

"I have her WhatsApp number. You can call her when we get to the albergue on WIFI."

Oh, these kids know all the technology tricks.

The three of us continue walking in a comfortable silence, listening to the birds chirp and enjoying the vineyards that stretch out before us on either side of the road.

We find the albergue soon after we walk into town, but the door is locked. There are a couple of backpacks sitting on the doorstep.

"Who do these belong to?" Jackie asks Sister Sophia.

"Pilgrims saving their place in line. They must've gotten here early. Line your packs up here by the door, so when it opens, we will be sure to get a place to sleep." Sister Sophia turns to me. "Helen, you look a bit anxious. Is everything ok?"

"Well, I made a deal with Aino, and I want to see if I can find her. But I'm not sure I want to leave my pack here unguarded."

"Mom, leave your pack with me. I will get you a bunk. You go to the square and see if you can find Aino. You can text me where to meet you. We have plenty of time before dinner."

"Thank you, dear. I believe I will. Oh, but I don't know how to get there."

Sister holds up her guidebook. "Here, in your guidebook, is a map of the city. We are here and this is the square. I suggest you look for Calle del Laurel, a pedestrian-only street with wonderful places to gather and eat. Just go down this street, turn left and you will get there. If you get lost, ask anyone and they will guide you."

"But I don't speak Spanish. I had no idea how dependent I am on you, Sister. I was so proud of myself for branching out. But, actually, I haven't."

"Ah, Helen, you are quite capable. You will figure it out."

"Thank you, Sister," I tell her, but I'm not confident she is correct. I start in that direction, praying for the best, but Camille has come back to the entrance of the albergue and she stops me.

"Where are you going, Helen? I want to show you the children's game at the plaza next door. It's so clever."

"I need to go find Aino, but I guess it can wait a second."

"But what about these?" Camille motions to all of our packs.

Sister tells her to leave the packs here in line.

"But won't someone steal them?"

"Now, who would want our dirty pilgrim's clothes and toothbrushes? We have our valuables on us. Everyone knows what a pilgrim carries in their pack and is respectful. They are safe," Sister says. "And we will be almost in eyesight of the door. Come on. Let's go to the plaza and I will tell you the history."

Camille, Jackie, Emily, and I follow Sister Sophia and Hannah down the alleyway to the church. There, embedded in the stone of the Plaza de Santiago, in front of the Iglesia de Santiago, is a huge mosaic containing sixty-three squares with geese, churches, a labyrinth, a prison, and a bridge. There are huge dice around the edge to sit on and watch the game.

"This is called the *"Game of the Goose"* and it is played with dice," Sister explains. "One progresses in a sacred spiral through the sixty-three squares. If you land on death you must go back to the beginning. If you land in prison you must wait there until someone releases you. If you land on a goose you get to move forward again as many squares as are on the dice. The game dates back to 1574 when it was gifted to Phillip II by Francesco de Medici, ambassador to Florence. It is believed to be much older, probably from ancient Greece or Egypt." Sister's depth of knowledge is remarkable.

"It's very symbolic," she continues. "Some games have the sacred stops on the Camino in the squares. The goose is a symbol of rebirth and fertility. The Way is full of symbology. Symbols that have been borrowed and transformed from all over the world to make them relevant to the Camino experience. Some believe that the goose footprint represents the sacred feminine."

"Amazing. Can we play?" Hannah asks.

"Well, I don't have any dice and it looks as though our albergue is opening." Sister gestures back at our accommodations. "Maybe later. Let's go stake out our bunks and get cleaned up. I understand you have a celebration to attend."

They all go to the albergue, and I make my way to the plaza. It looks so modern, yet so old-world. And there are so many people. How on earth am I going to find Aino?

"Divine guidance," the soft voice says.

I wander around the shops bordering the plaza. What I wouldn't give for some ice cream. I'm a grown woman with money in my pocket. There's no one to tell me whether I can have ice cream or not and what it will do to my figure. Besides, I've probably walked off every one of those calories today anyway.

I walk over to the shop I'd been eyeing and say, "A scoop of mint chocolate chip, please. In a cup."

"*Sí, señora.*"

"*Gracias.*" I'm starting to believe I can do this.

I make my way out to a bench to do some people-watching and eat my ice cream. The families are remarkable. All the different generations spending time together. I see a couple of older gentlemen sitting in front of a bar playing dominos while their grandchildren are playing a game of tag in the square. Their parents sit at the bar, keeping an eye on all. Next to them, there is a table of sophisticated young women drinking wine, talking, and watching the young men pass by. A vibrant community. It feels so good to be alive.

"Helen. *Hola.*"

"Aino. Hola." I look up in surprise, all these people and she finds me. "I am so happy to see you. I didn't want to welch on our deal."

"Welch?"

"That means to go back on, not follow through."

"Ah, yes, you Americans have such strange sayings. It is such a difficult language. Let us have a glass of wine and celebrate our meeting. The wine of this region, Rioja, is some of the best in the world."

"Well, I just had some incredible ice cream. I don't think I should splurge anymore."

"And why not? You are on holiday. Pilgrimage. If you want wine, drink wine. If you do not want it, do not drink it." Aino shakes her head at me. "You Americans and your puritanical ways."

"Puritanical? Now that's a big word."

"Well, the Puritans came to the United States from England. There's a lot of religious history there. They believed that the Church of England had strayed, and they wanted to go back to the Bible in its purest form. I believe they became a bit rigid."

"You sure know a lot about religion."

Aino shrugs. "I studied it. There are many believers in hospitals. It is important to treat my patients according to their beliefs."

I can no longer find a reason to argue the point. "I do believe I will have a glass of wine. Wine has a biblical and historical root. I can't be in the heart of wine country and not sample it."

"Come, I know the perfect cafe."

"I better text my daughter first and let her know where we are."

"Yes, please invite her along with the rest of your group. We will celebrate the woman."

"Isn't it early in the day for a celebration?" I ask.

"I did not know there was a proper time for a celebration. Besides, later we must check into our albergue, and get ready for mass and dinner. *Carpe diem!*"

"Oh, my goodness, Aino, you are going to be the death of me."

"Oh no, Helen, I bring life!" Her enthusiasm is contagious.

We stake out a large table close to the street so our group can find us. We order wine, and a plate of *pimientos riojanos*.

"Now be careful," Aino warns when the waiter brings our order. "For the most part the peppers are mild, but every now and then you get a hot one."

I nod and see the other ladies approaching. "Oh, there they are. Come and join us. Where is Sister?"

Jackie pulls out the chair next to me and sits. "She had a meeting with the priest to prepare for mass this evening. Those look yummy, what are they?"

"They are fried peppers. Aino says to beware. You may get a hot one!"

"Ooo...I like a hot one," Jackie says with a wink as she fills up everyone's wine glass.

"Celebrate. *Kippis!*" Aino shouts. "That means 'To your health' in Finnish."

"Kippis!" we all shout in return.

Aino waits until we've all taken our first sip, then says, "Did you all know that Spain, despite being full of Catholics, has a rich history in the sacred feminine? Especially the West Coast. It has its roots in matriarchal society. Have you ever wondered why there are so many statues of Mary? It is because of the respect for women. The pay is not quite equal, but better than most countries. Domestic violence is not tolerated. It is a perfect place to celebrate the feminine."

"Kippis!" Jackie shouts and we all laugh and toast to Spain and the sacred feminine.

"Oh, Aino, thank you for such a lovely celebration. You're right. Anytime is the right time for a celebration," I say as I spontaneously pull her in for a hug.

"You are welcome!"

The time passes too quickly and before I know it, Camille is on her feet, laying money on the table for the check. Aino picks up the money and puts it back in her hand. Insisting on paying she pulls out her credit card.

"Ladies, we need to get back, cleaned up and ready for mass. It's getting late," Camille says. "Thank you, Aino."

"Where are you staying tonight?" I ask Aino.

"With you of course." She links arms with me, and we make our way back to the convent.

Hannah scored me a bottom bunk and Aino takes the bottom one next to mine. I shower quickly as the water is not very hot, get dressed, and wash my few pieces of laundry. Hannah had already done hers. I finish just in time to meet the group in front of the door to the convent office.

Tora steps forward and greets me.

"Tora, it's so good to see you again. Did you ever get your pack from the airline?"

"Yes, it caught up with me in Pamplona. I'm so glad to see you all and return some of the things you let me borrow."

"Oh, thank goodness. I bet you're anxious to get them out of your pack." I have learned quickly that pack weight is no joke.

"Yes, it's heavy enough," she says, taking it off her back. She walks through the open door to the dormitory and drops it by an empty bunk.

The priest calls us to attention with a prayer and then explains that we will be going to the church through a secret passageway. He says this way had been used for centuries, not only to go perform the services but to spirit people away who were hiding from invaders.

We go through the old stone passageway. The stones gleam in the dim light. They have been polished by thousands of pilgrims throughout the ages. I can feel their presence in this place and am honored to be counted among them.

As we file into the church, the priest motions for us to sit in the front pews. Sister is already in her place by the pulpit. She starts interpreting as the priest says Mass in Spanish. We are then invited to receive the host. As we make our way to the altar, Aino kneels at the end of the communion rail. The priest offers her the wafer and wine. She takes the sacrament. Is she Catholic? But she said she is a lesbian. I will have to have a discrete conversation with Sister about this.

After the service, we make our way to the community dinner. They eat so late here in Spain, I'm glad we had an afternoon celebration. Aino sits next to me at the table. We all join hands and say grace. After dinner, the priest leads us in singing *Ultria et Susia,* I am so glad Sister taught us the words. The dinner, the company, the service, and the singing were all just delightful, but we turn in early. Tomorrow is a thirty-kilometer day.

Oh my, how am I ever going to keep up?

CHAPTER 9

LOGROÑO TO NÁJERA

Walking out of Logroño, we go through a tunnel under the highway, into a park surrounding a lake. People are fishing on the shore. A father is teaching his son to cast his line. A grandmother is pushing a baby stroller along the concrete path. I feel such joy watching the families.

The path starts up a hill alongside the highway, but there is a chain link fence separating us from the traffic. Pilgrims have scavenged grass and sticks to weave crude crosses through the links. I stop and think about all the things I am grateful for this morning.

Camille stops beside me to catch her breath. She and I are bringing up the rear once again.

"It's wonderful to see the faith so alive," she says.

I turn to her, smile, and ask how she's doing. She tells me that the blisters on her heels are almost a thing of the past and hopes they stay that way. I confess to a blister starting to form on my fourth toe.

"Let's take it easy," I say. "Though we have a really long walk today and I don't want us to hurt ourselves."

Camille shakes her head. "That's an advantage of being with Sister and Emily. They'll be there by lunchtime and will save a place for us."

"So much for Emily's intention to slow down. At least we can take advantage of her speed," I say with a nod. We walk on in silence as we head up the next mountain.

In the next town, we run into Hannah and Aino sitting at a sidewalk café.

"Hey Mom, Camille, how goes it?"

"May we join you?" I ask.

Hannah laughs. "Of course, take a load off!"

"Oh, it feels so good to take this pack off." I rub my shoulders and sit down next to her. "So, this is Nájera. That mountain was not as bad as I thought it would be. Where are we staying?"

"Seriously Mom? This is not Nájera, and that hill was not Alto San Antón."

"What? You mean we are not there yet!" I can't believe what I'm hearing.

"Mom, this is Navarrete, and that hill was Alto Grajera," Hannah rolls her eyes, a skill in which she has much proficiency.

"I know darling. I was just being hopeful."

"Oh, my goodness," Camille exclaims. "We've only gone twelve kilometers! Coffee, please, and one of the pastries with the chocolate inside. I'm going to need all the energy I can get."

Aino comes up behind me and gently touches my shoulders. "She's right. Where does it hurt?"

"Right here on my collarbones, where the straps press on them," I explain.

"You need some more padding there," she tells me.

"I don't know what I have that would make a pad."

Hannah points at my scarf. "How about that? You've been carrying it for days, why not make use of it?"

Aino agrees that it's a good idea.

I dig the scarf out of my pack, then put the pack on my back. Aino wraps the scarf several times around each shoulder strap. The concentration on her face makes it clear that she wants to get it just right. I can feel a flush as her fingers brush my breasts.

How silly of me. She is just wrapping a scarf!

"Now you are going to have to unwrap on one side to take your pack off. How does that feel?"

"So much better. Thank you, Aino." It is better. It's like someone just took the pain away. I can feel a warmth spread throughout my shoulders and neck. I tilt my head and the softness of the wool caresses my cheek, like a mother soothing a child.

There's a whisper in my ear. "You are enough, my child of God." Startled, I look up, but Aino has moved away and joins the rest of the group walking out the door. I hurry to catch up with them.

"I'm glad that worked." Aino says, looking at her handy work. "Come on, we have a long way to go. You may want to stop at the market across the street and pick up some snacks and water. There are no more places to eat between here and Nájera,"

Hannah speaks up. "No worries. I went to a market while waiting for you and Camille. I have cheese, bread, and grapes for all of us. We'll celebrate at the top of the mountain."

"Oh Hannah, I did something right when I brought you into the world."

The unexplained voice once again whispers in my ear. "Yes, you did."

I must be more tired than I think.

Camille claps her hands and addresses us all. "Well ladies, we are burning daylight as they say back on the farm in Missouri. Let's go."

I shake off the eerie feeling and start walking. It doesn't take long for Aino and Hannah to get ahead of us. Since they promised to wait for us at the top of San Antón, they'll get to rest!

CHAPTER 10

AINO AND HANNAH ON ALTO SAN ANTÓN

Aino and Hannah lean into the next ascent, leaving the others behind. The farm track turns into a dirt path that winds its way through the forest. The trees arch in cathedral wonder over the path, protecting the pilgrims who have walked this way for millennium. Along the side of the path, there are small stone carrions, the significance of which only the builder knows.

"Hannah, what are your study plans for University," Aino asks once they are out of earshot of the others.

"Oh, I don't know. There are so many choices. How did you know you wanted to be a doctor?"

"It was something I always wanted. I would take care of injured birds and squirrels as a child. My father always took me with him out on the farm to assist with the birth of the calves. I was born into it. It made it easier to stay focused on my dream."

"My parents haven't really pushed me to choose a path.

My Dad tells me I can do anything I want to do," Hannah rolls her eyes. "That kind of leaves it open. And Mom keeps on me about getting married and having grandchildren for her like I was some cow to give birth on demand."

"Oh Hannah, your mother has been brought up in a strict culture of tradition and it is hard to conceive of a different way of being. She is open-minded and seems to have accepted me for my choices. This means so much. Give her time to realize you are not a child anymore and can take care of yourself. She just wants you to be safe and happy."

"Safe, yes, but at what price? I see how hard my father works. He's rarely home. I know he loves us because he provides for us and is kind. We have all the stuff money can buy. But sometimes I just want him."

"Yes, a doctor must put her patients first. It was the one thing that got between me and Emilia, my wife. She always made sure I was well taken care of, but I did not always return the same. She never complained, but I could tell that she was hurt by it," Aino says, a tone of regret in her voice.

"That's why I don't want to have children yet. I want to make sure I can be there for a family. It's a huge responsibility. And I really don't want to just be a housewife. I don't mean to throw shade on Mom. She takes care of everything at home but doesn't seem to have any other identity. Besides, I want a husband before children, and there's no one I want to hook up with. She stops her tirade. and turns to Aino. "Are you divorced?"

"No, Emilia died a couple of years ago. She had breast cancer, and I could not cure her. I have felt an emptiness in my life ever since. My heart has been fuller since I have been walking the Camino."

"Oh, I'm so sorry, I didn't know."

"It is alright, Hannah. Talking about it helps. I was silent for so long. I am supposed to be the tough doctor, used to death. Well, I have never gotten used to death. I feel like I failed every time one of my patients dies."

"Dad and I talked about this once. He said that it was part of being a doctor. You can't cure everyone."

"Yes, there are some doctors who can take it as part of the job, but I have trouble with that. It feels like a piece of me dies every time one of them dies. When Emilia died, I did not want to live anymore. That's why I started working in war zones. It has taken me a while to come to this realization. I had a close call that put not only myself but others in danger. I have to face this suicidal intention. This is the purpose of my Camino. Living again. Right before Emilia died, she encouraged me to live my life fully. It is time to honor that wish." Aino stops walking and looks at Hannah. "Oh, I am sorry I have made you cry."

"It's ok. I cry so easily. My Dad says I need to toughen

up, but I don't know how," Hannah says. She wipes her eyes and begins to play with the end of her braid.

"I wish I could cry easily. I have toughened up and I am not sure that is the best way either. Look," Aino points, "the summit of Alto De San Antón."

"We made it! It wasn't so bad."

"I believe we are 'trail hardened.' Let us rest and wait on Camille and Helen. I have some bread and cheese to share for lunch."

"Thank you. I have some incredible grapes. I don't know what I like better, the grapes or the wine. Look at that view. I have never seen so many vineyards in my life." Hannah says, as she pops a few grapes into her mouth.

"Yes," Aino says and smiles. "It is awe-inspiring."

CHAPTER II

NÁJERA

"Aino. Hannah," I call out as we make the summit and see them waiting for us. "Is this the last mountain before Nájera? It better be because I don't think I can do another one today."

"Yes, Mom," Hannah says, patting the top of the stone wall beside her. "Sit here by me, Mom. A little bread and water will put you right."

I sit down next to her on the hard stone wall. I'm relieved to stop moving for a minute. I take off my boots and socks and let my feet air out. The fresh cool mountain breeze with the musty undertones of the fields breathes new energy into my body.

"Bread and water. Are we prisoners to the Camino? I am beginning to feel like I have been subjected to hard labor," Camille says taking off her pack and putting it on the ground next to the wall.

"The Camino provides. Come join me." Aino laughs as

she points to a place on the wall next to her.

Camille sits down next to her and I feel a pang of jealousy. I have not felt that in a long time.

"Look at the view." Aino gestures to the land laid out before us. "Have you ever seen so many grapes in your life?"

"It is beautiful," Camille says. "Think of all the blessings those grapes bring. Wine for communion... Aino, I saw you taking communion, I didn't know you're Catholic."

"Yes, I was brought up Catholic and made my first communion when I was eight years old."

"I thought you were a lesbian?" Camille doesn't seem to have any qualms about being direct.

Aino begins to put the food away in her pack. "I am. Being a Catholic and being a lesbian are not mutually exclusive."

"The church frowns on people in same-sex relationships. Do you walk the Camino to resolve this issue?" Camille continues to prod.

"No, I walk the Camino for personal reasons. Being Catholic and being lesbian is not an issue for me, but it sounds like it is an issue for you." Aino fastens her pack shut, turns her back on Camille, and asks me how my shoulders feel.

"Much better. Thank you, Aino. The scarf really did the trick. I do need to rest, though. That mountain was tough,"

I pretend I didn't hear Camille's comment as I don't want to take sides.

"You slayed it, Mom," Hannah says following my lead.

"Well, I made it to the top anyway."

Hannah hugs me. "You are tops in my book."

"And in mine," echoes Aino.

"So how much further do we have?" I ask.

Aino, her back still turned to Camille, answers. "Only eight more klicks."

"Klicks? Oh yeah, kilometers. So that's almost 5 miles. Ugh." I put my socks and boots back on. "Aino, would you help me wrap this scarf again to pad my shoulders."

Camille gives us a disgusting look, shoulders her pack, and starts down the mountain.

We all watch her stride away and then Hannah says, "She's such a Karen."

"Hannah, we taught you better than that. Everyone is allowed to have their own opinion." She rolls her eyes as we all start down the mountain.

Not much later, Hannah points and yells. "Hey, you all. Look over there. That's the memorial where Roland slayed the Muslim giant, Farragut, with a rock, and freed Charlemagne's Knights in the 12th century. Wow, people have been fighting wars for a long time." She says, walking and reading the guidebook at the same time.

Aino nods. "It is very sad that we try to settle our differences with violence. We must learn a better way."

"Yeah, what a waste. Just imagine where we would be if we put our minds to creating peace." Hannah stops for a sip from her water bottle.

"Do all young people in America feel the same as you do about war?" Aino asks. "Americans seem to always be in a conflict."

"My friends and I talk a little about war, but what we are really worried about is shooters. You never know when it's going to happen. I feel lucky that it's never happened in our school. We want gun control. I suppose there are times and places for guns and to stand up for what you believe in, even to the point of violence, but not senseless killing."

"Daughter, you have grown up," I say as we catch up with Camille.

"Mom, remember after the shooting school in South Florida, you and Dad were so concerned for our safety. We had a family meeting and talked about what we should do if it happened in our school. The boys and I talked afterward and decided you and Dad are dope!"

"It saddens me that we had to have those conversations. We should be talking about homework, boyfriends, and colleges."

"Yes," Camille chimes in as she rejoins the group.

"We have been discussing school shootings in church and it is so important to get back to strong family values."

Aino begins to herd us. "Come on ladies, Sister said we need to be present for evening mass at the Monasterio Santa Sophía De la Real, so we better get going."

Camille stops and looks at Aino. "What is the Monastery famous for?"

Hannah speaks up instead. "Well, the guidebook says that in 1156 a man was out hunting with a falcon and stumbled upon a cave with a statue of the Virgin Mary, so they built a monastery and a church." She stops walking and looks at me. "Wow, it is so hard for me to wrap my head around how old everything here is."

"Hannah, you're really getting into the history."

"Yes, Mom, history was so "snorrendous" in school, but here it comes alive. Like, people actually walked here thousands of years ago, real people who made the history books. It's not a fairy tale. Their blood and sweat actually soaked into the path we are walking on."

"Well, that's a bit gruesome to think about," Camille adds.

"Well, yeah, but it is real." Hannah picks up her pace to join Aino.

"I hope Aino is not putting any reprehensible ideas into Hannah's head," Camille says to me as Hannah gets out of earshot.

"Reprehensible? Heaven's no! We've taught Hannah to be open-minded, but to also think critically and make her own decisions. She has a good head on her shoulders. I don't believe Aino would do anything to hurt her." I turn and start down the mountain, wondering what, exactly I want for Hannah. And does it even matter? She will walk her own path. It's hard to let her go, but I must trust the foundation Ken and I gave her.

"Yes you should," the soft voice says.

CHAPTER 12

NÁJERA TO BELORADO

Leaving Nájera, the mountains turn into rolling hills, with vineyards popping up on each side of the gravel track. The new green grapes soaking up the sun to make that lovely wine. The farmers are out in the fields, nurturing them to get the best out of their crop. It's so peaceful. As we top another rise, I can see the gravel track winding into the distance, leading up to another mountain.

"You can do this," the voice whispers in my ear. *You can do this,* becomes a mantra that repeats itself in perfect rhythm with the crunch of my boots on the gravel track. "Yes, I can," I reply in kind, realizing that there is no one close to me to hear my response. Oh my. Am I losing it? They say if you answer yourself, you're crazy. Or is this the voice of the saints I wanted to hear? No, Helen, get a grip. I'm probably dehydrated. Yep, that's it. I just need to drink more. I stop, pull my water bottle out of my pack packet and take a long sip.

Aino and Hannah are in the distance, with Camille making her way alone behind them. I am once again bringing up the rear.

I can feel the water seeping into the parched cells of my body, I must have let myself get too thirsty. I'm going to have to be more careful. Putting the bottle back in my pack pocket, I remember Hannah's comment about it being like we are walking through a history book that is coming alive.

Sister shared that we are staying the night in Santo Domingo de Calzada. She told the story about a pilgrim couple and their son. A local young lady from a rich family takes a shine to him, but he does not return the feelings. She feels slighted and seeks revenge by putting a silver cup from her house into his pack and then accusing him of theft. He is tried and hung. His parents, with no recourse, continue walking towards Santiago in grief at the loss of their son.

Yet a miracle happens, and justice is done. He does not die. As legend has it, the parents return from Santiago and find their son alive, still hanging from the rope, by the grace of Santo Domingo. They go to the sheriff who is eating dinner, tells him their son is still alive and asks that he be released. The sheriff says he doesn't believe them. He said the boy is as dead as the chickens on my plate. Then the chickens come to life and fly off his plate. From then on, live chickens have been kept in the church.

I think about the two ladies on the horse. The young lady in the story was definitely from the shadow side. Women can be jealous and full of revenge. I remember a few catty girls from high school. I was never in that crowd.

I was surprised by my feelings when Camille confronted Aino. But I was justified, there is no call for rudeness. I got the feeling Camille wanted to string up Aino for being lesbian. Aino's actions are between herself and God and it's not Camille's place to be sheriff.

"What is your shadow side?" the soft voice said. I've never been a jealous person. In fact, Ken has never given me a reason to be jealous. That comment Hannah made about the amount of wine I drink at home went straight to the heart. Is my dark side the desire for wine in the afternoon when it gets too quiet at home? I never thought much about it before.

"Could it be loneliness?" the voice suggests.

I think about the white face, the face I show the world. Ignoring the soft voice in my head, I believe I am kind, tolerant, and supportive of others. Aino says she sees a light in me. Hannah questions me about my passion. I love being a mother. But is there more?

"Mom."

I look up at my daughter. A young man is standing

beside her. I was so lost in my thoughts that I didn't notice him until now.

"I want you to meet Ruben, he's a pilgrim walking without any money. Isn't that incredible? He's from Puenta La Reina. You know the town with the Queen's Bridge built in the 12th Century. That's where the knight fought for the love of a lady, remember?"

"*Encontado,*" I say in my poor Spanish, nice to meet you, as I look him over carefully.

"*Encantada,*" his reply respectful.

"He's staying where we're staying tonight at Santa Maria in Belorado, and he's offered to cook dinner."

"That's nice. What are you making?"

"*Sopa. Necessito vegetales.*"

"I am sure we can come up with some vegetables to make soup. I'll ask Sister. Where are Aino and Camille?"

"Camille caught up with us and tried to preach to Aino. She wasn't having it. I just dropped back and left them to it. I decided to wait for you, and that's when I ran into Ruben."

Hannah and Ruben's pace is slightly faster than mine and I see them communicating in Spanish, English, and pantomime as they continue along the way into town.

Sister is waiting for me at the door of the albergue. Ruben and Hannah have already gone in. "Sister, may we talk a minute?" I ask.

"Of course, this looks to be serious."

"Yes, it is. I just met young Ruben, who according to Hannah is walking without money and has offered to cook us dinner tonight."

"Yes, there are displaced young people on The Way. These small communities and farms do not have enough jobs for the young ones, especially the young men who are not the oldest son. There is still a hierarchy in place. The oldest gets the farm, the younger boys must fend for themselves. The cities call them, but they can't compete with those who have grown up there. Some employers recognize the Compostela on a resume. Having walked the way shows you are determined, strong, faithful, and can complete an arduous task. Ruben, I believe, looks to be one of those boys." Sister smiles at me. "I see you have not taken your eyes off of them. I believe Hannah is safe. Ruben is just lost. He has offered to cook as his contribution tonight. We will gather our resources and buy the necessary groceries. We take advantage of these opportunities that arise for us on the Camino to give back."

"Thank you, Sister. I would be pleased to contribute to dinner."

I enter the albergue. It is a parochial, connected to a church, where we stay for a donation. After a volunteer checks me in, I am directed to the women's dorm. That's a benefit of staying at an albergue run by the church. The rooms aren't co-ed. Hannah is already reclining on her top bunk and points to the one beneath her for me.

After settling in, Emily, Sister & I head to town to buy groceries and see the sites. There is this incredible mural with birds on the face of one of the buildings. I love how the Spanish turn everything into a work of art. We pick up enough vegetables, bread, and wine for a feast. When we get back, Ruben chases us all out of the kitchen and starts preparing his "famous" soup.

The laundry sink is outside in a lean-to, on the side of the building. The building butts up against a cliff and there is a steep path with a wooden railing leading to a fortification at the top. The Spanish sure knew where to build their fortifications to protect their towns. I am glad it is in ruins and no longer needed.

After hanging up my clothes, I go back inside. Delicious smells are emanating from the kitchen. Some of the other pilgrims are setting the table and writing in their journals. I sit in a soft chair by the wall and let the warm peaceful ambiance waft over me. Closing my eyes, I drift into quiet meditation where all is right with the world.

Father Pedro comes in and invites us to gather around the table. He gives the blessing for Ruben's soup. I dip my spoon in and the smell of garlic assaults my nose. It enhances the flavor of the vegetables. The *hospitalero* offers me a popsicle for dessert. A perfect ending.

After dinner, we all follow Father to the church where we sit in the choir, close to the altar. He gives us each a paper in our language with the prayers and order of mass. We take turns reading when he indicates to do so. After mass, he asks each of us to share a song from our faith. "Amazing Grace" erupts from my lips, and all join in their own languages. Hannah grabs my hand and sings harmony to my melody. She whispers in my ear, "We did good, Mom." Love fills my heart as I hug this very special child of mine.

It's leftover bread for toast and coffee for breakfast. We make our way out of town. Ruben had already left. He had his own path to walk. I hope he finds his way. The Camino is so interesting, people join us, move on, or fall behind. Some seem to have an important role to play, and some are just moving through. It's a mystery why certain people show up at certain times. Like Aino, what role does she have in my life?

CHAPTER 13

AINO & SISTER
SAN JUAN DE ORTEGA TO BURGOS

"Aino, I am so glad you joined us for mass last night," Sister says.

"I am too. I lost my faith in God after Emilia died, and working on the front lines has not helped to restore it." Aino pauses a minute to let the rest of the group get ahead of them.

"You are welcome to join our group," Sister says as they start walking.

"Thank you, Sister. I believe I will. There is something very special about this group,"

"Tell me about Emilia," Sister says, knowing they cannot be overheard.

"She was beautiful. We met in college, in biology. She was into research. She was always more at home in the lab with her mice than out with other people. She would join me to entertain our friends, but I could tell when she had enough. I was always the more outgoing one. Her mission was to find a cure for Alzheimer's. Her grandmother had died of the disease. She was a passionate soul." Aino stops. There is a tear slipping down Sister's cheek. "Oh, Sister, I did not mean to make you cry."

"It is fine. Truly. My heart hurts for you in your loss."

"You accept me?" Aino asks, surprised by Sister's compassion.

"Yes, we are all God's children. I noticed you take communion."

"I believe we are all accepted by Jesus, and I don't think he would deny me the host." Sister nods and Aino continues. "At home, my priest was of the old school of thought and when he realized that I am a lesbian, he refused to give me the host. I would go up to the rail and kneel anyway. He would say a blessing over me, but would never provide the host, even though I held my hands out. I was so furious. Emilia and I never kept our relationship a secret. On this pilgrimage, I have not advertised myself as a lesbian, but I have also not denied it either. It feels right for me to take the host." Aino's face is flushed.

"As you know, the church frowns on homosexuality, and I am uncomfortable with it also. It goes against everything I was taught." Sister adjusts her veil. "But I have learned much in this world, and I am not sure where I stand on this issue. Don't get me wrong, I respect your choice, but I just don't know about you taking the host."

Lifting her chin in defiance, "Jesus said, 'Suffer little children, and forbid them not, to come onto me: for of such is the kingdom of heaven.' Jesus accepted those children as they were. I, too, am a child of God. I too suffer. Shouldn't I be allowed to have the comfort of the body and blood of Christ."

Yes, he did. But—"

"I am sorry, Sister. I take the host because I can. Because I need to strengthen my faith. I have seen too much of war and suffering Sometimes I lose faith in a loving God. There was a time when it was easy to believe, but no longer." Her hands ball up into a fist.

"Oh, Aino, so much anger."

They climbed Alto Cruceiroin in silence, as a wet fog descended. The Cruz de Matagrande emerges out of the fog, a huge cross on top of the summit. At the foot of the cross, they see the rest of their group walking in circles, through a stone maze.

"What are they doing?" Aino asks.

"They are walking the labyrinth. This stone labyrinth has been at the foot of the cross for ages. Many pilgrims stop and walk it. The labyrinth originated in Greek Mythology as a maze, it was built for King Minos of Crete as a prison for the Minotaur. The King would send his enemies into the labyrinth to kill or be killed. No one survived until Theseus came along to save his people and kill the Minotaur."

"Go on," Aino tells her.

"When Theseus arrived in Crete, he met the daughter of the king and they fell in love. She gave him a spool of yarn to take with him into the labyrinth so he could find his way back out. He tied it to a post at the entrance, went into the maze, killed the Minotaur, then followed the yarn back out, married the princess and the rest is history."

"How does that relate to the church?"

"The labyrinth was adopted by the Catholic church in the medieval times as an alternative for those who could not afford to go on pilgrimage. It is not a maze, as there is one way in and one way out. You don't have to solve it out like a puzzle. It is built so you can move through it step by step mindfully. You don't have to worry about where you are going, so you have time for contemplation."

"So, the church can take myth and turn it into something sacred," Aino says, irony in her voice.

"You will need to try it for yourself and see. An American woman helped to revitalize the labyrinth in the 1990's, her name is Lauren Artress, and she wrote a book named Walking a Sacred Path. She likens walking the labyrinth to St. Theresa of Avila's path to God. There are three parts. The first is going into the maze. This is purgation, a time to release the things that do not serve you and keep you from serving God." Sister looks directly at Aino as she says this. "The center of the maze is illumination, where you can receive divine wisdom. Coming back out of the labyrinth you do so in union with God. It is very much like the Camino process. I suggest you try it."

Aino steps into the labyrinth and slowly makes her way to the center. In the center, she falls to her knees and prays. She is a long time getting up and walking back out. She then joins Sister, and they walk on in silence.

CHAPTER 14

BURGOS

As we approach Burgos, we take the alternate route through a beautiful park to avoid the industrial part of the city.

"Interesting," Hannah says as she confers with the guidebook. "Not only does this city have an incredible cathedral, but it also has a museum of Evolution. I wonder how that happened?"

"No need to be sarcastic. I believe Catholicism and Evolution can live side by side."

"Wow, how progressive of you, Mom," Hannah says rolling her eyes.

"In fact, I would really enjoy going to the museum. We walked by the archeological site this morning at Atapureca where they discovered early hominids that lived over 650,000 years ago."

Hannah stops walking and turns to me with a stunned look on her face. "What...?"

"You know I majored in science. I took an archeology

course just because I found it fascinating. I was hoping to get to see the archeological digs, but I will settle for the museum." I smile at her.

"Why didn't you ever tell me you studied archeology? Here I was going on about it like it was big news. thinking it was totally out of your lane."

"I didn't want to influence you."

It's so fun watching her. Seeing the look of amazement on her face. I remember when I realized my mother was a person, beyond just being my mother. I guess that's when I grew up a little, and started coming into my own as a person. I thought I had invented the world, too.

"Maybe you did pick up a little more from your old Mother than you realized. But I knew it would be hard for me to make a living and I needed a secure career." Giving her a wink, I add, "that was before your dad came along and swept me off my feet."

"That's right. I remember camping in Chaco Canyon and that trip to Mesa Verde. It was so cool. We'll be staying here in Burgos for a couple of days. I would love to see the museum."

"Did you know that your father and I made a list of all the Indian mounds in Florida and saw them before you all were born?"

"Really?" Hannah says as we start walking again. I'm

easily keeping her pace with this flat terrain. We continue through the greenspace alongside the river, and come upon a playground, with a dad pushing his daughter on a swing. Hannah loved to swing, the higher the better. Her giggles would spread sunlight all over us.

A yellow arrow indicates that we walk past the Puente Gasset spanning the Arlanzón River then turn right to use the pedestrian bridge. I'm so glad to see that safety is taken into consideration. This rush hour traffic reminds me of home.

As we reach the other side of the river, the bustle of people at the kiosks, shops and cafes overwhelms me. The smell of food assaults my nose. I can't believe I'm hungry again, as my stomach starts to growl.

"Oh look, there's the rest of our group at that little cafe. And look at those incredible pastries. I love these little cafes along the river. I believe the whole population of Burgos is out enjoying this glorious afternoon. I hope Tampa develops its riverfront like this. It's so friendly."

"Hola, Helen and Hannah. Come join us," Sister calls to us.

"Hola, are these for anyone?" Hannah is eying the pile of pastries and croquettes in the middle of the table.

"Of course. Take a load off" Emily says with a wink, doing a Hannah imitation.

"Emily, you kill me." Hannah laughs as she grabs a croissant.

"I'm so looking forward to visiting the Cathedral, going

to mass, and seeing the grave of El Cid. Do they have a special pilgrim's mass, Sister?" Camille asks.

"Yes, this evening at seven. We will first check into the Divina Pastora alburgue and then we will join the nuns for dinner after mass," Sister tells her.

"Then I better eat some more to tide me over," Hannah says shamelessly, and grabs a croquet. "Tell me more about El Cid?"

"You saw his statue as we came into the city. He is very important to Burgos and to Spain. He was a knight who lived during the eleventh century. The Moors named him, "El Cid" which means "the Lord". The Christians referred to him as "El Campeado" or "the Champion"," Sister pauses to take a sip of wine. "He is one of our national heroes. He was revered by both Muslim and Christians alike and united Valencia. Since he was born close by, he is buried here in the Cathedral. We will visit his grave tomorrow when we tour the cathedral."

"That's so crazy that a city with a huge Catholic Cathedral would have a museum for Evolution and a knight who could bring together Muslims and Christians," Hannah says.

"Yes, amazing. The hand of God is in all of this." Sister smiles.

"Wasn't this before most people could read and write and think for themselves?" Aino asks.

"True. Once people learned they could read and interpret the bible for themselves, they started connecting to God in their own way," Sister explains. "But that being said, there is a strong foundation of scripture that tells us right from wrong. Whenever I start questioning where I stand on an issue, I seek out the wisdom of the priests who have studied the Scripture in depth. Look at the time. We must go check in and get ready for mass."

We shoulder our packs and start toward Divina Pastora. I stop to take in the majesty of the Burgos Cathedral dominating the plaza. The ornate spires draw my eyes up toward the heavens. The rose window, reflecting the glowing colors of the late afternoon sun looks down on me, the eye of God watching over me. The portico below is the beautiful mouth of God, welcoming me in, to hear His word. There is no doubt of the glory of God from this structure.

The huge limestone walls, darkened by age, emanate a feeling of safety within their confines.

The builders sure knew what they were doing. There's a flight of stairs leading up to the doorway, with a figure of a bishop raising his hand in greeting. Above the door, carved into the limestone, is Christ sitting above his twelve apostles, flanked by an angel, a bird, a goat, and a lamb. The detail of the sculpture is amazing. It looks so real. I try to put myself into the shoes of an ancient pilgrim, with very little knowledge of the world, coming upon this masterpiece. They had to believe that they were in the presence of God.

"Incredible, isn't it?" Aino says pausing beside me.

"Amazing! The time and money that went into building this blows my mind."

"I believe the money came from the wool trade. The campaign El Cid led opened this area to trade. It took over three hundred years to build the Cathedral. I am looking forward to mass tonight and to the tour. There is so much history here," Aino says.

"The wool trade? I had no idea that wool was important in Spanish history," as I pull the scarf from under my collar and rub its fine material. "I wonder if this scarf was woven from Spanish wool?" The wind catches the free end of the scarf and lifts it toward the heavens. My gaze follows it, seeing the rays of the sun illuminating the clouds. I gently reach for the loose end of the scarf and tuck it into the collar of my jacket.

The whispering voice says, "You are a child of the earth and sky, trust in yourself."

Aino speaks and breaks my focus. "Are you alright, looks like you went away for a minute?"

"Oh, I'm fine, I just need to rest. What were you saying about the scarf?"

"I was saying that it was probably woven from Spanish wool and the colors were made from the natural elements of the earth. It perfectly reflects who you are."

"Hmmm... are you are joining us?" I say, changing the subject. This is just too weird. A talking scarf and Aino echoing its words.

"Yes, Sister invited me to officially join you and I accepted. Serendipity. I came on this Camino to have time alone for self-reflection and I have found so much more. I am so grateful that I met you."

"We are blessed to have you join us. You have so much to offer."

"Aino, Helen, this way," Camille calls to us.

"Oh, we better hurry up and join them," I say to Aino.

"Let's have breakfast together tomorrow."

"I would like that. I'd like to learn more about Doctors Without Borders."

"I would like to learn more about you."

I can't seem to rest this afternoon. Leaving every-one else napping, I walk around the old town by myself. It's so lovely that they don't allow cars in these old city centers. It feels like I've walked back on time. Time, yes, it's so precious. Seeing Hannah and the boys growing so fast, it's just slipping away. Though sometimes in the afternoons at home, after all my chores are done, I feel like it's standing still.

I drop to a bench with a statue of a worn-out pilgrim sitting at one end. His clothes are tattered, and he holds a staff and gourd in his outstretched hand, preventing him from falling off the bench in his stupor. I wonder if I will look like that when I get to Santiago.

Everyone seems to have a personal goal, a purpose, except me. Yes, I came on this trip to support Hannah in her transition to adulthood and make memories but maybe there is more.

"There is," the soft voice says.

Yes, Hannah was right. I do have a glass or two of wine to ease the loneliness. All my friends do it too. We get together to play cards, and the wine flows. But I wonder if it's an excuse to drink. But I know I am not an alcoholic.

With determination, I stand up and adjust the scarf around my neck. You silly old scarf, you really aren't talking. It must be part of the self-reflection process Sister is always going on about. Day after tomorrow we enter the Meseta. Maybe I will have a spiritual revelation there.

I wander down one of the stone streets, looking at shops that could have been here since medieval times. I stop in front of a shop with bottles of wine in the window. Looking at the scarf, I ask it, "Do I need wine to make it through the afternoon?" It doesn't reply.

There are afternoons I didn't drink, especially if I'm driving carpool. No, I don't have to have it, but it sure is relaxing. Ken has never said anything about it, and this is the first time Hannah has said anything. I bet the boys never even noticed. "Catholics drink wine and so did Jesus," I say, trying to convince the scarf of my sobriety.

The wind catches the end of the scarf and points me back to the square, to the Cathedral. The arched entrance is beckoning. I stop in the first chapel and do a double take. There is a life-size crucifix above the altar. Is that human hair on the Christ and real blood dripping from his wounds? I read the sign at the entrance. Yes, real human hair but the blood is paint. It's gruesome. Yet it's an image to make Christ more human, to bleed and to suffer. We want Him to feel what we feel. We want Him to know our suffering. We even rejoice in his suffering. We feel hope in His resurrection. He had to leave the body to become one with God.

I hurt for his mother, watching him die. I can't even imagine. Sister says that's why the Spaniards revere the Virgin Mary. She knows the suffering of a mother. She knows that things happen to children over which a mother has no control. She never forsook her son, and neither will the faithful of Spain.

I sit in a pew in front of the crucifix and say a rosary in honor of Mary, her Son, and their suffering to give us life.

I hear our group quietly chatting as they come in for mass, in the main nave. I get up, cross myself, and go sit next to Hannah. I just have to touch her, knowing that one day too soon in the future she will be off exploring the world on her own. Taking risks, finding love, advocating for others, and possibly suffering and dying. All those things we do as humans. It is just so hard to let her out from under my protective wing. I can't even imagine what it must feel like watching your child die.

CHAPTER 15

REST DAY BURGOS

"I'm so glad we have a clear sunny day for sightseeing and resting," I say to Aino at the front door of the albergue, commenting on the lack of cars on the streets.

"Yes, this is usual in Europe. We maintain our heritage by keeping the old parts of our cities intact. It is so delightful to be able to enjoy our treasures and relax at our cafes. Let's go find some chocolate and *churros*."

"What are churros?" I ask.

"A fried dough pastry. We dip them in hot chocolate. It is delectable."

"Sort of like a donut?"

"Well, I have never had a donut, but I have heard some of my American colleagues talking about them," Aino locks arms with me and leads the way through the plaza.

"I believe there is a place by the river. It would be so nice to sit by the water," I suggest, a bit uncomfortable with this intimate arrangement. I unhook my arm and look at the ornate facades of the buildings towering over me. Taking a deep breath and releasing it, I follow Aino as she leads the way through the ancient city gate, towards the river to a café.

I pause as we walk under the archway of the gate. "I can just imagine in medieval times, the knights and their ladies riding through the gate and carrying their standards. What an incredible display that must have been," I say.

My eye is drawn to the river. What perfect planning to fortify the city. Enemies would have to cross the river and then make it through the gate. But now there are no such barriers. Across the bridge is a park with a fountain, children already cooling off in its spray on this warm morning. The modern facade of the Museum of Evolution is as imposing as the ancient gate to the city on this side of the river. Office buildings and storefronts grace the new avenues. The old and the new exist together in harmony.

"I could fancy myself as a knight in armor on a white horse," Aino says, assuming a 'knightly' pose.

I take her up on her fantasy. "And me a damsel, with scarves of silk flowing off the tip of my hat." Laughing as I wave the end of the scarf to the masses. "But I have no idea how the ladies stayed on those horses sitting side saddle."

"I believe I would have been one of those women who wore pants, sitting astride, and causing gossip," Aino replies.

"You know what they say. 'Well-behaved women, never make history,'"

"Are you well-behaved?" Aino asks, raising an eyebrow.

"Yes, I tend to go with the status quo."

"The what?"

"I tend to do what society expects. There are parts of me that would like to rebel, but I guess I'm a chicken."

"I don't believe that. Here we are," Aino pulls out a chair for me to sit on and sits down next to me as the waiter appears. She orders for us.

"Oh, thank you for ordering. What a treat. You know it's heaven not to have that pack on today."

"What do you want to do today?" Aino asks.

"Well, I promised Hannah a trip to the Museum of Evolution and, of course, we must officially tour the Cathedral and see El Cid's grave. I would like to peek into the stores and see what they sell here. Not that I want to buy anything, I don't want to put anything else in my backpack!"

"I understand, but a small souvenir of our time together would be nice," Aino smiles at me. I can feel the warmth of her gaze coursing through my body.

"Tell me about your work," I say, changing the subject, a bit uncomfortable with the direction of the conversation.

"My specialty is infectious disease. But now I do just about anything that needs to be done. I am stationed at a small clinic in Afghanistan where we serve a local refugee camp. The clinic was a school for girls, that is no longer being used, because of the current regime."

"It sounds so primitive."

"Yes, but we make do. We have a few hospital beds set up in the common room of the school and we use the classrooms as patient care rooms. And for the small pharmacy, it is housed in a closet."

"How do you get the medicine?" I ask.

"It is bought by donations and transported to us by the military. The toilet facility is a latrine in the back of the school. We are lucky. We have a well and a stove so we can boil water and prepare food."

"I suppose you have to boil all of your water." I take so much for granted.

"There is a small home next to the school where we live. I am the only doctor and I have three nurses working with me. They are amazing and can make anything out of nothing.

"Oh, Aino, how do you manage?" I see the frustration and pride reflected in her face.

"If it is more than we can handle we transport the patient to a larger hospital. We treat everything from malnutrition to minor gunshot wounds. We give vaccinations, do prenatal care, labor and delivery, but mostly we provide a safe haven, some food, and triage."

"You are their first hope." I smile at her.

"I guess you can say that. There are so many needs, that it does not give me time to think. I do what I can to alleviate the suffering, and sometimes it is not enough."

I put my hand on hers.

"You would be amazed at the spirit of the people. I helped deliver a breech baby and we were able to save the mother and the child. The husband brought us a chicken for our dinner. That chicken and some rice made a nice soup to feed our patients and staff for several days. It is these gifts and moments that make it all worthwhile."

"I was training to be a labor and delivery nurse. Do you think there would be a place for me?" I ask, my shoulders straightening up in pride.

"Oh yes. My heart goes out to these women. There is very little birth control and sometimes they get pregnant, not by their own choice."

"I just can't even imagine how hard it is to be a woman in that situation. I so admire the work you are doing." I squeeze her hand.

"Thank you. It has become a passion, but with passion comes burnout. Constantly being on call with so much need, you feel like you cannot even begin to fulfill it. I want to be clear with you. It is a tough job. Not like working in a first-world hospital and going home to a good meal, nice home, and family."

"I've never seen, much less worked in conditions like those. I would be willing to see if I could. I want to make a difference."

Aino gives my hand a squeeze back. I can feel the strength and the warmth in that grip. That warmth in my body cranks up a few more degrees as a flush overcomes my face.

"There they are, and what is that?" Jackie asks as she walks up to our table. "It looks sinful." I quickly snatch my hand away from Aino's and turn to smile as Camille and Hannah have also now come around the corner.

"Where are Sister and Emily?" I ask, trying to recover my balance.

"They are visiting with the Cistercian Nuns. Emily has expressed interest in the order and Sister is making it happen." Camille says.

Aino shakes her head. "Sister is remarkable. I feel like we have only scratched the surface of her wisdom."

"Jackie, this is chocolate and churros. They're like little donuts and this chocolate is not like the hot chocolate from home. You can stand your spoon up in it," I point to the extra chairs at the table.

"Join us." Aino moves her chair closer to mine.

"Oh, thank you. I hope we're not intruding," Camille looks at me with an accusing gaze.

"Of course not. We were just discussing Doctors

Without Borders and Aino's work on the front lines. It makes me feel so mollycoddled,"

Hannah laughs. "Mollycoddled! That's a new one on me, Mom. Dad has sheltered us from the world. In some ways, I feel very blessed and in other ways, I want to break out and experience it for myself. So, Mom, are you going to volunteer?"

"Well, I would have to go back to nursing school and improve my French. It could be done." I shrug.

"Yes, you can do it," the voice says.

My head jerks in response. So, it's still following me. Hannah looks at me with concern as panic spreads across my face. I regain control of my face and smile at her.

"Of course you can," Jackie says. "We are women – hear us roar!!"

Hannah orders more coffee, chocolate, and churros, and then takes out the guidebook. "Look, the museum is right across the river, and it opens at ten. That's in fifteen minutes. Let's go there first, come back, have lunch, and then visit the cathedral."

"A perfect plan." Aino looks at me and smiles. I can feel the warmth of her smile all the way down to my toes.

CHAPTER 16

THE MESETA:
BURGOS TO CARRIÓN DE LAS CONDES

"That was such a lovely service last night," Camille remarks as we make our way out of the city onto the flatter terrain of the Meseta.

Sister told us last night that we are embarking upon the second spiritual phase of our Camino, the great high plain of the central region of Spain. All I can hear in my mind is "The rain in Spain stays mainly on the plain." I'm not looking forward to walking in the rain, but today seems to be an exception, as the sun is already hot on my head. Mary shared with me her experience of a rainy Meseta, the mud clinging to her boots, sucking her feet into the earth, each step a chore. I hope I don't have to experience this.

I look at the colors in the scarf, tucked under my pack straps the way Aino suggested. The reds, blues, oranges, pinks and purples are the Camino. What a comfort to know that it has traveled this way before. Mary said the scarf needed to come back to the Camino, but I still don't

know why. So far it has provided me warmth and cushion-
ing for my straps.

"You know why."

I look around. Camille is walking and talking with Aino,
and there is no one else close. The breeze is winding its way
through the vineyard. I can feel it caressing my face. I stop
and let it ruffle my hair, lifting the fringe of the scarf.

"You know why," the voice insisted.

Is the scarf here because I'm here? I came for Hannah,
but the scarf wasn't given to Hannah. I never even thought
about sharing it with her. Mary gave it to me. It's mine.
There are so few things that are really mine.

Ken paid for the backpack, my clothes, and the trip. He
pays for the roof over our heads and the utilities to keep the
house functioning. The money in the bank account he made.
Yes, I have contributed my blood, sweat and tears to make
it a home. I have been a wonderful wife, but is that enough?

"You are enough," the voice whispers.

Nobody else is questioning this. Ken feels the money is his
contribution. Mine is the labor. The kids see it as seamless.
They never question where the finances come from. Why is
this important to me? I never even thought of it before.

But Camille, Emily, Sister, and Aino all have jobs. They
also have the same other responsibilities that I do. Well,
some of them don't have children, but Camille and Jackie

do. I'm very blessed to have a husband who takes care of me financially. I am so grateful for this opportunity. But did I earn it? I look at the scarf and it does not have an answer to my question.

Oh my, now I'm listening to the scarf!

"Helen," Aino calls out to me. "If you are waiting for the grapes to turn into wine, you will be standing there a long time."

Snapping back to reality, I wave and quicken my pace to catch up with them. The Meseta is not flat. I see the rolling hills stretch out before me as I make my way along the gravel farm track. Topping a rise, I see the next town in the distance, but then it disappears as soon as I think I am upon it. A cruel game of hide and seek. And all I can do is keep moving forward. What was the word Sister used? Ultreia.

Aino breaks the silence. "Beautiful, so lush and fertile. I look at all these poor villages and contrast them with the opulence of the cathedral. I wonder if the money would have done more good providing for the parishioners."

"Yes, I too, have thought about that."

"A cathedral is to glorify God, make the people feel close to heaven," Camille says rebuking them. "It shows our love and devotion to the church. It's a treasury for all to come and experience."

"You have a point, Camille," I say. "The artistry and the devotion are so evident. I'm sure it provided hope, jobs, and spiritual sustenance to the community."

Aino shakes her head. "You can't live on spirit alone. The other thing I oppose is the gold. It was gotten on the backs of slaves and indigenous peoples. There is an ugly history that is covered up by the excesses of the few. I am not proud of that part of Catholicism,"

Camille agrees and then says, "But the splendor that came from that is God's will. I don't agree with the methods of the conquistadors or the Inquisition, but I do know that we are to bring the faith to others. Paul wrote about this in 2 Corinthians 10:5-6:

> 5 For we are overturning reasonings and every lofty thing raised up against the knowledge of God, and we are bringing every thought into captivity to make it obedient to the Christ; 6 and we are prepared to inflict punishment for every disobedience, as soon as your own obedience is complete.

It's important to be obedient to God's will and bring others to the Glory of God. The cathedrals are proof of that glory," Camille concluded.

"Inflict punishment? I don't remember that in the bible," Hannah says.

I chime in. "I can see that the cathedrals give hope to all the parishioners. It's the physical representation of the Glory of God. It gives them something to look forward to for their labor,"

"I have seen too much power-mongering and the pain it evokes on the masses," Aino says. "I admire the craftsmanship and the artistry, but I cannot help but think of all those who suffered for it."

"But we suffer in life as Christ suffered. It's when we reach heaven that we will rest in his glory. We need to spread the good news to all," Camille adds.

Aino counters. "I believe that because of my faith, I have been given a gift to alleviate suffering, not evoke it,"

"I'm glad we've grown beyond the Inquisition and the conquistadores and have a humane view of the world. It's part of my own faith journey to become more like Jesus and reach out to the poor and sick, offering healing and food. Look at the work of the nuns in Burgos. That's one reason I've started thinking about going back into nursing. I so admire the work you do, Aino."

"Your calling?" asks the soft voice, reminding me of our earlier conversation.

Now I'm even starting to think of the scarf as a real being.

Aino smiles at me in gratitude.

We continue walking, the only sound breaking the silence is the never-ceasing crunch of the gravel farm track under our feet. I can see green shoots starting to peek out of the furrows of rich earth, merging into a green haze that stretches towards the horizon.

Hannah pauses beneath an ancient arch over the road and calls to Aino and me. She reads the plaque on the side of the crumbling wall. "This is the arch at the ruins of San Anton."

A symbol in the shape of a 'T' piques my curiosity. We wander over to join the rest of our group taking a break in the shade at a fruit stand.

"It is a tau cross," Sister explains. "It is known as the pilgrim's cross, Cruz del Peregrino, and is worn to protect against illness and sickness."

"I need a bunch of these to take back to Afghanistan," Aino tells her.

Camille looks surprised. "Oh, you're going back?"

"I have been giving this a lot of thought. I am not sure," Aino says. "I don't know if this work is my calling me or an excuse to run from life. I have time to figure it out."

"Come and enjoy the fruit." Sister motions to us. "If you would like, the proprietor will share the meaning of your name for a donation. In Proverbs 22.1 it says, "A good name is more desirable than great riches; to be esteemed is better than silver or gold." "

"Well, Hannah," I say. "I know the meaning of yours. It has Hebrew origins and means 'grace'. You have definitely graced our lives,"

"Mom, what does Helen mean?"

The proprietor has joined us. He smiles and says, "Your name has Greek origins and means 'light'. That does not surprise me at all. I can see a light deep in your soul. You should let it shine."

I thank him and drop a donation in the box. There it is again, a light hidden deep in my soul, just waiting for me to let it shine. Nonsense.

"Maybe not," the voice says. I shake my head ignoring it.

We continue listening to our steps crunch as we make our way through incredible farmlands. Camille fell into step with me. We tend to pace about the same.

"How are your feet," I ask.

"Oh, so much better, thank you. And how's that toe of yours?"

"It's just about healed. Hopefully this terrain will keep it that way," I reply, feeling like our conversation has become polite and stilted.

"Have you thought any more about renewing your nurse's training?"

"Yes, actually I think about it a lot. I'll see what happens. What does the name Camille mean?" I ask her.

"It means 'helper to priest'. I have certainly lived it through my work in the church. I was brought up to serve. I even thought I would be a nun and studied for a while as a novice, but then I fell in love and got married. Sometimes, I regret not taking my vows, but my marriage was wonderful, and I have four strong young men and three beautiful daughters-in-law. I know they will take care of me as I age." Camille's eyes drill into me, "it's the way it should be. Have you thought any more about your marriage and future?"

"What do you mean, my marriage? My marriage is solid. And my future? This something I am trying to figure out."

"Well, I don't think it's a good idea to run off with Aino to Afghanistan."

"You are way off base," I tuck the scarf under the straps of my pack, feeling reassurance in its warmth, then I charge ahead in silence, leaving her in my dust. I don't have to hang around and be judged by her.

CHAPTER 17

CARRIÓN DE LOS CONDES

Life has been distilled down to eat, sleep, and walk, giving my mind free rein.

"Mom, welcome to Carrión de Los Condes," Hannah says when I get to the albuergue. I have already staked out a bottom bunk for you. Emily and Sister are making arrangements for dinner and the pilgrim's mass."

"Have you seen Aino yet?" I ask.

"Yeah, she's already showered and taken off for town. She said something about shopping."

Camille comes in behind me. "She's all about her fruits and vegetables."

I wonder if there was more to that statement than just produce.

Hannah continues, "Tomorrow we have to walk seventeen klicks before there is a place to stop and eat. I believe she's getting snacks for all of us."

"That's so kind of her. I'm so tired; I don't think I could

walk another step. Can you believe we have come over 350 kilometers? I really didn't believe I could do it and we're almost halfway there," I say.

"Well, I just looked it up in the guidebook," Hannah says. "The halfway point is at 366 kilometers and then we will stop in Sahagún and get our halfway certificate. Now go get cleaned up. The nuns are having a sing-along in the hall before the service. I hear there's something very special about this service."

"Yes, daughter!" I laugh. Is she already practicing to take care of me in my dotage?

I make my way into the front room where an impromptu concert has been set up. One of the nuns has a guitar and leads the singing. Sister Sophia is singing harmony. They talk about their mission to bring spirituality back to the church and the Camino.

After the music, we make our way into the Church of Santa Sophia del Camino. When the time comes for the pilgrims blessing one of the nuns stands. With Sister Sophia interpreting, she holds up a beautiful paper hand-colored stars and says, "The stars are very light, it is not a burden to carry, and will keep you safe in God's protection along the way and as pilgrims, you bring light to the world." The nuns give us each a star as we exit the church.

My light? What is the light I bring to the world?

"You know," the scarf says.

Well, I guess I can no longer deny it. The scarf is going to talk to me whether I want to listen or not. Mary said it talked to her, but I thought it was just an expression.

The next morning, we distribute the food Aino has gotten for us and fill up extra water bottles. I dig the scarf out of the bottom of my pack. The weather app on my phone indicates that it's about seven degrees Celsius out there. In America, that's about forty-five degrees. Cold for this Floridian.

I start wrapping the scarf around my neck as I walk out the door with the pack on my back. I feel in my pants pocket the star the sisters gave me last night. I smile when I feel the wax from the crayons they used to color the paper, to make its light shine.

"This is why you are here," the scarf says to me.

I draw in a deep breath and fille up my whole body with the morning light. Exhaling, I imagine the light going out into the world.

The end of the scarf lifts in the breeze, I capture it and s ecurely tuck it into the top of my jacket. Looking up, I see the next yellow arrow guiding me down the main street of the village. My footsteps carry me forward on their own volition out of the village, back onto the never-ending farm track.

As I top another hill, I turn to look back the way we came, and I see some of our group in the distance. I'm in the lead. Will wonders never cease?

Turning back towards the west and Santiago, I scan the area for yellow arrows. I don't have to think about walking and navigating more, it's automatic.

It seems like the rest of our group is giving me space. Or maybe they need their own quiet time too. I settle into the rhythm of my stride as the path gently rises.

There's always something to do for the kids or Ken. He's actually low maintenance, but there are still things to do to keep him healthy and working. And the house in repair because surgeon Ken is not very handy. He just doesn't to want to risk his hands and I understand that.

Yep, look at me. Not only can I cook, clean, and sew, but I can fix toilets and sinks, and maintain the pool, and yard. I can even paint and do some basic carpentry. I could hire myself out as a handy person, get a white van, and call my business "No Job Too Small for Helen!" or "Helen's Handy Woman Service." Now that has a nice ring to it. I give myself a pat on the back.

Ken would be horrified, not to say anything of the kids. I start giggling and quickly look around. I don't want anyone to think I'm off my rocker.

Looking down at the scarf, "Yep, that's why I'm here,

I'm off my rocker and I love it!" I take the scarf from around my neck and start waving it in the air like a ribbon, twirling and dancing to the crunch of my feet on the farm track. "Come one, come all, just call Helen. She will fix what ails you and your house. A one-stop fix-it shop."

I kind of like the idea of renewing my nursing license. "It won't be easy, you know," I say, looking at the scarf in my hands, slowing to a walk. I wasn't just making conversation when we were talking about me going back to school. I would have to learn to use computers and all the latest equipment. I did all right in school the first time around. I was in the top ten percent of the class. Math was easy, but chemistry and pharmacology gave me fits. All those pills and side effects. I'm sure there's a whole new crop of pills out now, with a whole new crop of side effects. Aino seems to think I can do it.

The scarf flutters in the breeze in agreement.

Aino has such a belief in my abilities, and she doesn't even know me. When I'm around her I feel adept and admired. The way her eyes light up when she sees me makes my heart sing. I have some good female friends, but I have never had a friend quite like her. There is a special bond and I've only known her for a few days. It almost feels like a lifetime. It must be a Camino thing.

I wonder what it would be like working with her. I'm

sure she would be kind and instructive. She has such a compassionate heart. As I'm thinking of Aino, I see her up ahead of me and I holler a hello.

"Hola, Helen. Join me for lunch."

"I do believe I will. It's still so cold. I thought it would warm up some. I am so glad to have been gifted this scarf."

"Me too. It looks good on you. The red adds a vibrancy to your complexion. In fact, you appear to be glowing."

We both take a seat on a stone wall at the side of the path. It feels good to sit.

"Do you want some of my bocadillo?" I ask, unwrapping the huge sandwich bursting with ham, Manchego cheese, tomatoes, pickled peppers, and aioli sauce.

"No, I just finished my apple and cheese.

"You know, I never thought I would love a sandwich as much as I love these. It sounds so silly. I know it's just a sandwich, but the bread is so fresh, and the local meats and cheese are so different from home. It fills me right up and keeps me walking." I realize I am rambling. "Have you thought more about your future?"

"I am not sure I can go back. The suffering is so much. I feel so alone in it. I have not connected with anyone at the clinic. Most of the young girls are flirting with the young men. Youth, even in a refugee camp in the middle of the war, takes comfort in concupiscence. It's in our biology."

"You make it sound so boring. 'Love is in our biology.'"

"Are you in love with your husband?"

"Do you mean all starry-eyed and obsessed? No, I don't think I ever felt that way. That's for the movies. What we have is steadfast. It's been that way for a long time. I have the children and he has the hospital."

"Steadfast. What about romance?"

"Romance at my age?" I laugh and adjust the scarf around my neck. "Jackie would have something to say about that."

"Jackie is right. I miss the romance in my life," Aino says. "I believe that is why the young ones at the camp seek relationships. It gives them moments of pleasure."

"Pleasure? I have not thought about that for a long time. I've been too busy taking care of the kids, Ken, and the home."

"What do you remember about pleasure?"

"It's the feeling of security that I remember and that has never wavered. I went from home to nursing school in the dormitory to being a mom."

"I don't mean to pry, and you don't have to answer, but do you enjoy your sexual relationship with your husband?"

"Oh, Aino, such personal questions. Did you enjoy your sexual relationship with Emilia?"

"Yes, it was an integral part of our relationship. We both loved to love. I really miss the intimacy. I have been pleasuring myself, but it is not the same. Now, your turn."

"Well, I don't dislike it. It's something we did to have the children. Ken is so tired when he comes home from the hospital. I guess we had a few moments on our honeymoon, but we were young and poor, and it was just a weekend. We both had to be back at work on Monday. Ken in his residency and me in my clinicals. I never thought about it much."

"Have you ever thought about loving a woman?"

"Well, I have never thought about having sex with a woman or a man, besides Ken. First, the church frowns on it, and I could never commit adultery. I believe adultery would constitute any sex partner outside of marriage."

"I understand. Emilia and I were monogamous. After she died, I dated some. But could not find the right fit, so I buried myself in my job. I am not so sure that is the right thing for me. I want my life to be whole."

"There are so many parts of us. I have buried some parts of who I am for so long I don't know if they exist anymore."

"It's sort of like the scarf you are wearing." Aino fingers the material around my neck. I feel a shock of electricity as she takes the wool into her hand. "Each strand is a part of us that makes it whole. Without one of those strands, the scarf would lose something vital."

"Yes, I know what you mean. As I was walking, I was

toying with the idea of having my own business. I have no idea where that came from, but it was fun."

"You know where it came from," the voice says, as Aino continues to examine the scarf.

"What kind of business?" She still has her hand on the scarf.

"A handywoman. I can fix just about anything."

"There are so many parts of you that are hidden," She continues to caress the scarf. "The Camino is incredible that way. It gives us a chance to take stock and possibly choose a new path."

I gently tug the end of the scarf from her fingers and start cleaning up. "Speaking of paths, we better get going. We have a long way to go."

We collect our things and begin anew. As we walk along the fields of green wheat, the growth in the past few days is remarkable. The smell of fertile earth wafts past my nose. The rows are so perfectly tended, quickening under the guidance of God's hand. Across the sky, puffs of white and grey clouds race by, playing hide and seek with the sun. The crunch of our boots on the gravel farm track takes us ever closer to Santiago. I don't want this to end. I could walk this road forever.

"How did you know you preferred women to men, Aino?"

"I am the child that liked playing outside with the boys

and working on the farm. I didn't want to stay in and do women's work. As I was growing up, I enjoyed my close women friends. I had one best friend and we experimented with each other. We were fifteen and trying to figure out sex. We had heard about how glorious it was and wanted to experience it. Getting pregnant wasn't a deterrent," She says with a wink. "As I got older, I did date a few men, but I never had that feeling for them. I was drawn towards women. Then I met Emilia, and it was love at first glance. I asked her out and a year later we got married."

"So, you always knew you preferred women?"

Aino turns and looks directly into my eyes. "Yes. I have some good friends who are men, but I have no interest in them sexually."

"I've always preferred the company of women to the company of men. I even thought about going into the convent. My parents wanted grandchildren, so I decided I should get married instead. They did insist upon me getting a career, you know, 'to fall back on.' I always wanted to be a nurse and knew I could make a living from it.

Then I met Ken, and we would talk about medicine. He belonged to our same parish. Because of his hospital duties, he rarely made it to mass. Once we got to know each other, he made an effort. Frequently, we would go to Sunday mass and then to brunch. He would then go back to the hospital, and I would study. It became a habit. We were comfortable with each other."

"But, how about your sexual relationship?" Aino touches my arm.

"We were comfortable with each other. We wanted children and we had Hannah. Then the twins were born eighteen months later. I had my tubes tied because their birth was so hard on me, and the doctors said I shouldn't have any more children. After that, we drifted apart. He was too tired from the hospital, and I was too tired taking care of twin sons. It just didn't seem important anymore."

"Not important? Intimacy is so important. It is part of being a human," she says as her hand strokes my arm.

"Oh, Aino. You are so passionate."

"Yes, I am. Do you feel it too, Helen?"

I can feel her eyes on me. A flush makes its way up my face and I can feel the heat rising from the scarf around my neck. I unwind the scarf, taking my arm out of her grasp. I fondle the soft wool and continue down the road, not knowing what to say.

CHAPTER 18

LEON TO VILLAR DE MAZARIFE

I make my way in silence into Leon. Even the scarf doesn't have anything to say. The cold industrial buildings make way for new shops and office buildings of glass. The yellow arrow points down a narrow side street of bricks and leads to the Albergue De Peregrinos de Las Benedictinas. Going through the arched entrance is like entering a small city. Pilgrims are hanging out in the courtyard doing laundry and soaking in the sun. There is a small group practicing yoga on the grass. I climb up the stairs, a small café to the right of the office contains vending machines with sustenance for hungry pilgrims.

I walk into the office on the left, check in with the hospitalero, and purchase a new credential. Mine is full of beautiful unique stamps from all the places I have stayed, the churches I have seen, and the bars in which I have enjoyed good wine and food. I'm anxious to fill this new one with memories as I make my way to Santiago.

With a new credential in hand, I climb another flight of stairs to a huge dormitory. The sleeping areas are on the left and the bathrooms are on the right of the center aisle. The hall seems to go on forever. The guidebook says there are one hundred and thirty-two beds. Sister beckons me to the end of the hall where there are seven beds cordoned off for our group. I put my pack on the floor and roll my sleeping bag out on a bottom bunk noticing an electric outlet on the wall. I scored, a bed with power is a prize catch in an albergue. Hannah is the on bunk above.

My group of women and I leave our laundry blowing in the breeze and make our way to the square and the cathedral. We wander through Barrio Húmedo, where many pilgrims are enjoying some of the best food and wine the city has to offer. We proceed down another small alleyway and the cathedral bursts into view. My jaw drops, I have never seen anything so magnificent. I thought the cathedral in Burgos was opulent. This cathedral is so much more.

We follow Sister inside for the tour. The nave is illuminated by a multitude of vibrant colors which radiate from the stained-glass windows lining the walls. I stand in the light in awe.

"You are light," the soft voice whispers.

I hug the scarf close, letting the light absorb into every part of my being. I want to rest in this light forever.

Camille breaks my meditation and encourages me to keep up with the group. I acquiesce to her guidance. As we walk through the nave and out into the cloister, the ambient light darkens. I smile, realizing that I have the secret of light in my hands and my heart. It is not in the windows of the church, but inside of me, and it is fueled by the love around me. The scarf is but a physical reminder to keep the light alive inside of me.

We walk through the cloister and come to the door of the museum. A docent takes our tickets and leads us inside.

"OMG, this is horrible," Hannah exclaims as we pass into a room of paintings. The images of women being tortured, and babies being murdered by priests, leap off the walls. I put my arm around her. She turns her face into my shoulder, and I hug her even tighter. She looks up at me and her face reflects the pain of the young woman in the painting. Hannah is about same the age of the woman being held down on a table in a dungeon and tortured by a priest.

I turn to Sister Sophia. "Sister, why are there paintings of the Inquisition here? "

"This is a period of history of which the church is not proud. But if we do not remember the past, we will repeat it. This is a reminder of what we as humans are capable. But we are also capable of great humanity and love. We must keep our dark side in check. That is why we profess our sins and do our penance. The Camino was originally a walk of penance. Those who sinned against God were instructed to walk to Santiago to be absolved."

"You are so right. 'Never again.' I remember seeing that sign in a movie about the holocaust," Hannah says, shaking her head.

"Yes, 'never again.' Jesus was about acceptance and love. There are no stories of him torturing people to bend them to his will. He would pray for them, heal and treat them with compassion. The Inquisition was an ugly time in our history." Sister lowers her head in a brief silent prayer and crosses herself.

"Why are Cathedrals so opulent? I thought Jesus taught that it was easier for the poor to get into heaven than the rich," Hannah asks. I continue to hold her in love.

"We show our God-given gifts and talents through the building of these places of worship. Those who come here get hope. They revel in the glory of God. Do you feel His presence within these walls?"

"Yes, Sister, I do feel a presence, a warmth. I feel safe and cared for. I feel love. even among this gruesome reminder of the past." Hannah smiles at me and then moves on to look at the next display. Her concentration on each exhibit astounds me as I follow behind.

Our group exits the Cathedral and walks through

the square. There are restaurants lining the parameter. Sister leads us into one. The waiter runs up to us, hugs Sister, and seats us all at a large table. He brings glasses, a carafe of wine, and a huge plate of calamari. Sister tells us that we will be leaving the Meseta tomorrow and the terrain will become more mountainous. This is spiritual the phase of the Camino. It is a time to integrate all you have experienced.

The next morning, we make our way out of Leon. The route out of town goes by the cathedral and through downtown to a large plaza. We stop by a stone column topped by a crucifix. At its base is a statue of an exhausted pilgrim. I sit down next to him, as a laughing Emily takes a picture of us weary pilgrims. The statue is in front of the Parador Hotel. It is one of a chain of luxury hotels in Spain. I understand they do have a pilgrim price, but I am sure it's not in our budget.

Emily grabs my hand and pulls me up. "Helen, may I have a moment?"

"Of course, are you still trying to slow down?" we walk across the plaza leaving the rest of the group taking pictures with the weary pilgrim.

"Well, I've about given up on that idea, but I can aspire

to it," she says, laughing. "But seriously, I've been talking to Sister about the role of women in the church. It appears things haven't changed much over time. As you know, we're still not allowed to be priests or even rise higher in the church. We are kept in the role of servant to the priest." She stomps her foot on the ancient stone in defiance.

"Is that what you want? To be Pope?"

"Well, yes and no. But I would like to take a more active role in the church. When I was initially hired as a computer tech, there were very few women as managers. It felt good to be one of the first and youngest promoted to that position. As time went on, I realized I was just as capable as everyone else. I loved that my company focused on capability, not gender. I would like to see the church take the same stance. There must be many women who could aspire to become not only priests, but bishops, cardinals, and even the pope."

I spot the next yellow arrow, directing us to cross a bridge over a river. I point. "We go that way." Picking up my pace to keep up with her.

I think about everything she just said, and I stroke the scarf. No, being Pope is not for me. I'm follower, not a leader. But Emily, yes, I could see her on the balcony at St. Peters waving to the masses.

"You're a radical," I tell her. "I like how you think. I've

only thought about expanding my role from mother and wife to getting a job. And here you are aspiring to be the Pope. I've always depended on others to put bread on the table. I don't even know if I would be able to do it, but I'd like to try,"

"I take it for granted. I've been earning my own way since I graduated from high school. I chose not to have a family, but to have a career instead."

"Did you ever have a special relationship?"

"Oh, I dated, but usually when we got to the point of tying the knot, I would get cold feet. I never had a strong urge for children. Did you have that urge?"

So, that's how she's been able to maintain her figure.

"Oh yes. I always wanted to have children. It was more important to me than anything else. I was lucky to find the right man who could both give me children and provide for us." Remembering Ken at home, looking after the twins, and working long hours causes a bit of guilt to grab me in the gut. I'll call him tonight when we get to the albergue.

"That's my point. When we feel the call, whether it's being a manager, a mother, a wife, a doctor, or a priest, there shouldn't be any artificial barriers." Her hands punctuate each word.

"I've watched Sister Sophia. She has the intelligence, negotiation, and financial skills to take any role in the church she desires. If she wants to be a bishop then she should have the opportunity to apply." I share her enthusiasm. Why not, as Jackie says, 'hear us roar'?

"I'm wondering how I could pave the way for the next generation of women to aspire to their dreams."

"What a wonderful idea." I look at the threads in the scarf. "What can I do to help?" Oh my, what did I just sign up for?

"I thought I would start in my diocese," she says. "Let's talk to Sister Sophia and the rest of our group. Maybe we can start a movement."

"It would definitely turn the church upside down." I'm imagining the fireworks when Camille gets wind of this.

"Do you think Aino would be interested? I see her taking communion, so I assume she's Catholic."

"Yes, she's Catholic. We could ask her. She seems to be a barrier buster."

"I like that. A Barrier Buster, pun intended."

"Emily! I didn't mean it that way. You are wicked."

"Emily wicked?" Aino says catching up with us.

"Yes, she's plotting a feminine revolt in the church. She's going to call us the Barrier BUST-ers." I laugh just repeating the phrase.

"I love it." Aino offers us a thumbs-up. "What barrier are we busting?"

"The patriarchy of the Catholic church," Emily pounding her hiking poles on the track increases her stride. I struggle to keep up.

I am awed being in the presence of these two accomplished women. I don't know if I can keep up.

"Yes you can," said the scarf reminds me.

"Count me in," Aino says, increasing her stride to keep up Emily. "I've always believed women were capable of more than setting the altar and arranging the flowers. In fact, nuns have been the unsung backbone of the church for millennium. I have read the Gospel of Mary Magdalene. The patriarchy in the Council of Nicaea wrote her out of the bible, and with her, women. They turned us into servants. I am fine with serving others but don't degrade me because I do. I believe we are all here to care for each other."

"Here, here! Barrier Busters unite." Emily stops, drops her poles and extends her open palms, inviting us to hold hands and we raise our arms to the sky in solidarity. Even the scarf gets into the act as the fringe catches on my arm and it flies up into the air.

Camille walks up behind us stopped on the path. "What is all this noise?"

"We have decided to become Barrier Busters and break through some of the patriarchal barriers in the church," Emily says. "There's no reason women shouldn't be allowed to become priests or ascend to whatever level they are called."

"The Bible doesn't condone women in those roles," Camille rebuts. "Therefore, I cannot condone this idea." Her posture stiffens and that no-nonsense expression appears on her face.

I step back to watch the debate.

"The Bible was written by men and maybe God didn't mean for it to be interpreted that way." Emily's fire was not about to be put out.

"But God gave the interpretation to man," Camille shakes her head, obviously determined not to lose the argument.

"Yes, so they say. Women weren't even allowed to learn to read and write at the time. I wonder what it would've been like if women had been allowed to be part of the decision-making." Emily resumes walking with us at her side.

We approach the intersection where Sister told us to turn left toward Villar de Mazarife. She said the albergue owner was a friend who would provide us with both dinner and breakfast.

I can feel my tendons stretching as I lengthen my stride. It kind of feels good. Who would have thought?

"Scarf, we're going to be Barrier Busters." I giggle. It does have a nice ring to it.

"Yes, you are", the scarf replies.

CHAPTER 19

ON THE ROAD TO VILLAR DE MAZARIFE

Aino, walking beside me in silence, doesn't notice that I spoke to my scarf. I don't want her to think I've lost my mind or maybe she would be good with it.

"With women in charge there would be more stories of compassion and less of war," she says. "That is one reason I like the New Testament better than the old. I love the compassion and healing of Christ. I believe this is the image in which we are made."

"Agreed," I say. Surprised at my conviction.

Camille shoots me a look that could kill. "I'll see what Sister has to say to you bunch of anarchists. I would not want the responsibility of a priest or the pope. It is a man's responsibility. I am here to serve."

"There are many ways of serving. We have a responsibility to humankind and the earth," Emily says. "I would consider going into the church in service if I had the opportunity to be part of making and enforcing the rules, instead of being treated like a second-class citizen. You may choose a different path, but at least you would get to choose. Not all men are leaders. Some are followers. We need all these talents to make a difference."

I'm definitely a follower. I've always shied away from leadership positions. Tell me what to do, and it's done. Reliable, that's me.

"And more," the scarf whispers.

"Emily, you will get no argument from me. I like being a doctor on the front line, taking care of patients. I would not want to be an administrator. That is not my gift. It should be about the gift, not the gender."

I see Camille stiffen and she turns to Aino. "You call yourself a Catholic, and I've seen you take communion, how can you sin like this?"

I knew it wouldn't take long for this to come around again. I going to have to take sides. Where do I stand?

"You know where you stand," the scarf says.

"I am a woman and I happen to have feelings for women instead of men. That does not make me a sinner. I believe we are all equal in God's eye."

"That's blasphemy," her eyes narrowing. I've never seen Camille so worked up.

"I disagree. It is blasphemy for a person to falsely judge another person. I do not judge your choice to prefer men.

It is just how you are biologically. We are all different and, in that difference, we are all needed in this world." Aino stops and turns to face Camille. Camille stops just short of Aino, her knuckles turning white as she clenches her hiking poles. They are almost toe to toe.

Emily and I pause and look at each other, ready to jump in if needed.

"You can use all the fancy words you want to, but I will not allow you to influence others to a life of sin. Helen let's go."

I just stand there in shock. Where does she get off calling Aino a sinner? The look of contempt on Camille's face is not unlike the expression on the face of the Inquisitor in the painting at the Cathedral.

Emily moves to next to Aino. "I stand with Aino. She has been kind and supportive. You did not turn your back on her when she tended your blisters. Sister invited her to be part of our group, knowing she is a lesbian."

I clinch the scarf around my neck. Camille and I are more alike than I want to admit, steeped in the tradition of the church. I didn't want to rock the boat as we walked out of Burgos, but I guess now I'll have to decide.

"Let it shine," the scarf says to me.

"I, too, stand with Aino." Joining Aino and Emily, we turn together and start walking again.

Camille being left behind calls after me "Do you know

where your daughter is and what kind of influence this will have on her?" Not wanting to let it go she comes after us.

"Actually, I do know where Hannah is. She also accepts people regardless of race, religion, gender, and sexual orientation."

"If you call accepting shamelessly flirting with those French men."

"Hannah knows how to set boundaries and I totally trust her. She's with Jackie and I know they're safe. Changing the subject doesn't negate the fact that we support Aino in her life choices. She's not hurting you." I say as calmly as I know how, not breaking stride.

Camille throws another barb. "And I see how you and Aino are together, it's shameful."

Ignoring her, I keep walking. I think about my Uncle Jim. He was brought up in the South. As a gay man, he kept his secret close never sharing with anyone in the family. There was a time when he abused alcohol and drugs, but he eventually he found AA and got sober. I was of a younger generation and more tolerant of his life choices. I think that's why he finally came out to me. I assured him that the family had already guessed and loved him just the same. He cried tears of relief and joy.

But as for me? I don't know. Is it biological? Aino has raised questions about my sexual choices.

"Yes, you do have choices," the scarf reminds me.

I look at the congruence of the colors in the scarf. The choices are not just black and white.

Part of me cringes at the thought of a woman as a partner. Is this because I have been carefully taught to feel this way? Part of me is curious what it would be like. At times I feel uncomfortable around Aino, like she wants more from me than I can give.

"Thank you for standing up for me," Aino says, startling me out of my thoughts. "I just could not be responsible for my reaction to that woman, if I stayed around." Smiling at us, she changes the subject. "Did you know that Spain, a country steeped in Catholicism, is one of the first countries in Europe to legalize gay marriage?"

"No, I didn't. But I'm glad to hear it. We have legalized same-sex marriage in the U.S., but there are still many people who would like to change that law and go back to the way it was. It's becoming quite controversial again. Along with the rights women have over their own bodies."

She slows her pace to walk with me as Emily charges ahead. "Yes, I follow the politics in your country. I believe the patriarchal part of society is seeing the handwriting on the wall and giving one last hard push to maintain control. I hope those who are more accepting of everyone's freedoms and liberties can come out on top. It must be hard to live in such tumultuous times."

"Yes, it is, but I believe it has awakened a movement that had become apathetic, me included. I hadn't even considered that we would go backward. It scares me for Hannah, potentially losing the choice over what happens to her and her body."

Emily enters the town ahead of us and I see her stop in front of a café. As Aino and I catch up, she smiles and offers to buy us a cup of coffee. We sit at a table facing the road and see Camille approach. Emily gets up and meets her on the road, handing her a fresh cup of coffee. She invites her to join us. Yes, she would make a good Pope.

CHAPTER 20

VILLAR DE MAZARIFE TO ASTORGA

The next morning, we leave Mazarife to walk the twenty-eight kilometers to Astorga. The threatening overcast sky makes good on its promise. Each of us cocoons in our ponchos and slog our way over the rolling hills, through farmland and forest. Jackie and Hannah quickly get out in front. Emily, true to her word to slow down, sticks with Aino and me. Sister and Camille bring up the rear.

A lean-to materializes out of the gloom, next to an old ruin with a table laden with snacks. Above the opening is a sign that reads La Casa de los Dioses Cantina. Jackie and Hannah are already sitting in the shelter, munching a snack.

I drop money in the donation jar and grab a banana. Mana from heaven straight to my stomach.

"Astorga. This is where chocolate was first introduced to Europe," Hannah reads from the guidebook.

"I love chocolate, almost more than I love sex. And that's saying a lot."

"Oh Jackie, it's great to hear you talk about your marriage and the relationship you have with your husband. I hope one day I find a man that I can love in all aspects."

"I hope you do too, darling. Never settle for less. I am proud of the way you handled those men from France. They are too precious, but it would only be a fling."

"It's fun to flirt, but you're so right. I'm not interested in a fling or the potential consequences of a fling. I have a lot of adventure to look forward to first. It's been fun practicing my French with the guys. I believe I could get good at it. Maybe I could be a tour guide or a writer."

I could feel my heart sing, so proud of this daughter of mine. Emily catches my drift and winks at me.

Sister Sophia walks up to our table and asks if we have seen David, her friend who created this garden of plenty for pilgrims.

"We haven't seen anyone," Hannah tells her. "But the sign is welcoming, and we are hungry pilgrims,"

"Eat your fill and leave a donation for David. He has been blessing to pilgrims with his hospitality for years. I'm sorry not to see him on this trip. As soon as you are all done, we must go. The rain is supposed to get worse as the day progresses."

Hannah motions to me that she is going ahead with Jackie and Camille while I finish my snack. I wave her on as I drop my peel in a compost bin. I walk over to a crumbling wall and peek over. I see a well-tended garden. I look around for a toilet, but there isn't one. I grab my 'pee pack ' and find a hidden place to squat. After I am done, I put the used tissue into one of the disposable doggie bags Sister encouraged us to bring. I tie up the bag and deposit it in the trash can.

Hurrying, I catch up with Aino, Emily, and Sister as they start down the muddy farm track.

ASTORGA: CAMILLE, HANNAH, AND JACKIE

"Hey, Camille, Hannah, over here." Jackie jumps over a torrent of water rushing down the gutter and ducks into a chocolate shop.

"Come on, Camille. Jackie says it is almost better than sex," Hannah says and leaps over the torrent and to join Jackie in the shop.

"What is this preoccupation with sex?" Camille screws up her face in disgust and follows them. "There's more to life than sex. And all this feminist talk. Can't people just be good Catholics?"

Hannah looks at her, surprised.

"Whoa, girl. Where did that come from?" says Jackie.

"Oh, you two weren't there. Aino, Emily, and your mother," she points at Hannah, "are plotting a feminist revolt in the Catholic church and letting homosexuals take communion."

"When did this happen?" Hannah asks and takes a step back.

"I'm so glad you don't know anything about this heresy, child. Your mother is being led astray by Aino and Emily. I thought Emily would have more sense. And your mother just blows with the wind."

Hannah takes a defensive stance. "That's my mother you're dissing, and you have no right to say anything against her."

"Well, you have no idea what she is up to. She's probably trying to protect you. What did they call themselves... the Barrier Busters!"

"Lawd have mercy, the Barrier Busters. What kind of barriers are they busting?" Jackie laughs, her blue eyes twinkling.

"They think a woman should be allowed to be Pope if she wants to, and she has no problem with you cavorting with those men from France." Camille waves her hand to emphasize the point. "Do you have any idea what men from France like to do to women?"

"Those men from France have been perfect gentlemen. And what's wrong with a female Pope?" Jackie interjects.

"I wouldn't want the job myself, but I think it would be wonderful," Hannah turns her back on Camille to peruse the display cases.

Jackie walks over to Camille and gently touches her on the arm. "How about some chocolate? It might be just what you need. This is the chocolate capital of the world, and I can't wait to taste it. My treat."

"*¿Senoras y señorita, quieren chocolate? ¿Están peregrinas?*" the shopkeeper asks.

"*Sí,*" Jackie confirms that they are pilgrims and want chocolate.

"I have a little English. Where are you from?"

"We are from the United States," Hannah tells her.

"You are in *el primero* chocolate shop in Spain. Do you want anything special?"

"The best chocolate shop in Spain?" Hannah's eyes light up. "What's this one?" She points to a delectable confection. "We are tired and hungry pilgrims."

"Dark chocolate with nuts and caramel. We also have chocolate filled with strawberries, mint, oranges, or nuts, dark and milk. What is your pleasure?"

"I'll have that one," Hannah tells him.

"I'll take the strawberry filled," Jackie says. "Camille, what will you have?" leading her to the display case.

"I'll take the milk chocolate."

The shopkeeper gets their choices, rings them up, and hands Jackie the bags. Camille takes her bag out of Jackie's hands and walks out of the store The rain is taking a break, and a weak ray of sun is peeking through the clouds.

CHAPTER 22

ASTORGA

I spy Camille on the sidewalk in front of a chocolate shop. I know where my daughter is.

"I thought I would find you with the chocolate," I say as Aino, Emily, Sister and I walk into the shop. "What's Camille doing standing on the sidewalk, looking like she lost her best friend?"

"More like dissing her best friend," Hannah says. "Come get some chocolate. It's incredible."

"It smells incredible and remember we're going to the chocolate museum later so don't ruin your appetite," I say.

"Being a pilgrim works up the appetite. I'll buy some for the next few days," said Aino.

"Mom, can we chat for a minute?"

"Of course, let's get our treats and go sit in the square."

We find a marginally dry table with an umbrella covering it. I smooth my poncho over my bottom to protect my pants from the damp seat. "You may be interested to know that the building across from the shop is the Bishop's Palace, designed by Gaudi. I would almost rather see that instead of the chocolate museum," I say, my mind going a mile a minute.

Hannah turns to see what building I'm talking about. "It looks awesome. I bet Sister wouldn't mind if we did some exploring on our own."

"We'll ask her when she comes out of the shop. So, what do you want to talk about?"

"Mom, Camille just said some horrible things about you. Well, I don't think they are horrible, but she does. She said you are committing heresy by advocating for women to be priests and approving of Aino taking communion. She said you are allowing me to run wild. I wouldn't have it. What's up?"

"Oh my, thank you for standing by me. Camille is very traditional in her beliefs. This doesn't make her good and me bad, or vice versa. It means we have different beliefs. I've been trying to be supportive of her beliefs, but also of the other women. We need to find some common ground." I unzip my jacket under my poncho and loosen the scarf from around my neck, letting the heat dissipate.

"That must be why she said you "blew with the wind.""

"Probably. I've been looking at my personal beliefs and trying to determine where I stand. I'm leaning more and more towards women having the same opportunities as men in the church and life. I, too, was brought up traditionally, but I'm open to new ideas. And I kind of like the idea of women asserting their roles in the church. Sometimes 'blowing with the wind' can mean you are looking at other options and haven't made a decision yet. What are your beliefs?"

"It wasn't on my radar. Going to church was just something we did as a family. I have some great friends there and love singing in the contemporary band, but God and Jesus and all those stories, seem like just that – stories. Seeing the cathedrals, the museums, and the holy shrines have blown my mind. Sister was right about the Meseta."

She squeezed the rain out of the end of her dripping wet braid. "Since the French men ghosted us, I've had time to think. There's something to this spiritual thing. I just don't know yet. I guess I'm blowing in the wind too. I don't like all patriarchy in the church and, wow, do they ever revere virgins," Hannah glanced away for a second. "You and Dad have been really clear about no sex before marriage. But this is the 21st century, and with the pill, we do have choices."

"And what have you chosen?" I'm wondering if this child of mine is a virgin.

"Jackie and I talked; she promotes monogamy. She said that when a guy tries to put the moves on you, you have to decide if he is worthy of you. I love that. I know that Dad is worthy of you, and I bet you have never compromised your self-respect."

"You're right. I never compromised my self-respect," I lean forward and catch her gaze. "Now, that's not to say I haven't been tempted. There are some good-looking sweet talkers out there. I was very sheltered. We didn't have the same freedoms that you have today. I get concerned about that. I also get concerned about someone taking advantage of you. Men are physically stronger, and biological drive can circumvent good sense,"

"Yes, André was really cute and there was this energy between us. He loves to travel as much as I do. I was glad at times you or Jackie were close by because it stopped me from accepting some of his more serious flirtations," she smiles at me.

"Now you understand why they had chaperones in the olden days. This was the only 'protection' women had. One incident of unbridled passion could lead to years of regret. I want you to have the freedom to grow into a confident woman before you have the responsibility of children."

Hannah paused and a furrow appeared on her brow. "Do you regret getting married so young and having children right away?"

"I never questioned my decision. I'd been sheltered

in some ways, but my time as a nursing student opened my eyes to the results of other life choices people make. It was expected of me to marry and have children. No regrets. I love you and the boys and being a mother. And I'm very proud that maybe I've had a little influence on how well you have turned out." I touch her arm and smile, to make sure she knows how much she means to me. She leans forward and gives me a soggy hug.

"I just love this. We have so many more options than you did, and I'm aware of how hard women had to fight for them. I want to be part of the movement. There is no reason Emily shouldn't have just as much of a chance of becoming the pope as a man. And Aino be allowed to take communion."

I raise my hand for a high-five, and we say together, "Barrier Busters."

Laughing, Hannah turns her attention to the guide-book and reads about the Bishop's Palace aloud. "There is a painting on display of St. Agatha, the patron saint of breast cancer. I bet Jackie would like to see this."

Sister Sophia comes out of one of the shops and waves to us.

"Oh look, there's Sister. Let's go talk to her about going to the Bishop's Palace."

It's not going to be an easy painting to look at.

I remember Saint Agatha from Bible study. But I can't shelter her forever. I zip my jacket and tuck the scarf back under the collar.

"Knowledge is wisdom," the scarf whispers.

CHAPTER 23

ASTORGA TO FONCEBADÓN

The next morning, the sun is out early and so are we. Just a couple of klicks out of Astorga we come upon a park with a small chapel built over a well. Many of these churches are built over ancient sites with flowing water.

I walk into the chapel, put an offering in the donation box, and pull out my credential. The volunteer by the door puts a stamp on it and motions me over to the well. In a book on top of the well these words are written:

A legend tells us that a little boy fell down this well.

The mother in her despair, begged to the Ecce Homo: Jesus Christ, save him!

And the little boy came back to the mother's arms healthy and saved.

> You, who walk in your life, with the water of
> this well, make the sign of the cross.
> And may Jesus be with you, deliver you from all
> danger, and after all your sacrifices,
> may you arrive happy to your destiny.

I take some of the water from the well and cross myself. I am so blessed. My children are healthy in my arms.

We walk across the street to a park and Sister gathers us under a young maple tree. The plaque on the ground says:

In loving memory of Denise Pikka Thiem,
a beautiful soul
5 April 2015

Sister recounts the story of Denise, a young pilgrim aged forty-one, from Arizona who was murdered on the Camino. She was diverted from the main Camino by following fake arrows to a nearby village. The arrows were painted by a hermit to lure pilgrims to his property. He assaulted her and buried her body. Later he turned himself in. He was found guilty and is serving time.

After Denise's death, the people of the village, pilgrims, and the church prayed over the area and cleared all the negative energy. The people who live along the way continue to be watchful. Pilgrims are a great economic boost to their country, and this is a sacred walk.

The memorial was erected in her memory and serves as a remembrance of others who have died on the Camino. Most die of sudden heart attacks or illness. But death is rare, and the civil guard is very alert to the safety of pilgrims.

The memorial reminds us to watch out for each other. Our Father said:

> Two are better than one, because they have a good reward for their toil. For if they fall, one will lift up his fellow. But woe to him who is alone when he falls and has not another to lift him up! Again, if two lie together, they keep warm, but how can one keep warm alone? Ecclesiastes 4:9-11

After Denise was murdered, a Facebook page was created called *"Camigas – A Buddy System for Women on the Camino."* I love the name Camigas. The group was created because many women want to walk their pilgrimage alone. The fear level of doing this increased when Denise went missing. The *Camigas* Facebook page is a way for women to connect and support each other in fulfilling their dream of solo pilgrimage. We are here to 'lift up' each other. Anywhere in the world, you must be alert and aware, but Spain is one of the safest countries in the world in which to travel.

After Sister shares all this information, the group of us walks on in silence. It's so sad to think that people who come here to accomplish a life's dream may lose their lives. People die all the time. I just didn't think of it in this context.

I grab onto the end of the scarf, thinking of my own mortality and vulnerability. I've never worried about my death. I've been frightened for my children. I worry about them when they're not under my wing. It's just a Mom thing. Denise's family must have been beside themselves. I hurt for their loss.

"I'll always be here for you," the voice whispers.

I am finding so much solace in the voice. It was never part of my life before the Camino, I am glad to know it will always be with me.

Sometimes, I wonder how I will die. I always thought it would be in my sleep, but that's not reality. I hope to leave a legacy. To make the world better for my children and generations to come. Kind of like the rule I learned in Girl Scouts, "Leave it better than you found it."

"You are," the voice says.

The rain continues on and off for two days as we make our way up into the mountains. Each of us is lost in our own thoughts. Entering the town of Foncebadón, we find our albergue. Sister leads us around back where we shed our ponchos and muddy boots on the back porch. I look at Jackie and start to laugh. Her blonde hair is sticking out in all sorts of directions. I grab the ends of my hair and imitate her doo. She hugs me laughing and we start to lose our balance on the wet floor.

"Ladies, ladies," the hospitalero admonishes. "You must be careful. Come in and get dry. I have hot chocolate and pastries."

Jackie and I regain our balance and with our arms around each other, we make our way into a cozy common area with a huge roaring fire. Sister sits down in a rocking chair next to the hearth and motions for us to join her.

"Tomorrow, we will get up before dawn and walk two kilometers up the mountain to Cruz De Ferro. You have each been carrying a token that represents your purpose and/or burdens for this pilgrimage. It is time to offer the token and all it represents to God. We will have a prayer together as the sun rises. Then each of you will have private time at the cross to release the burdens you have been carrying with you. You may want to take some time this evening to prepare," Sister says.

After dinner, we make our way up to our dormitory. I don't have many problems or burdens, I thought getting ready for bed. When I look at the state of the world and the people around me, what I am carrying is so little. Folding the scarf up into a pillow and placing it under my head, gratitude flows through me.

"Have you figured out why you are here?" the scarf asks.

"I'm here for Hannah," I whisper back.

Someone across the room shushes me. I didn't realize I'd been talking out loud.

Trying to find a comfortable spot on this horrible mattress that pilgrims have been sleeping on and doing God knows what since the 12th Century isn't easy. I settle back down to sleep.

The scarf intrudes again. "Have you figured out why you are here?"

"I told you why I am here. Just leave me alone and let me sleep," I respond silently.

"That is quite noble of you, but there is more." The scarf isn't going to let me sleep.

I take it from under my head, ball it up, and toss it to the foot of my bed.

"You said you wanted to hear the voices of the saints and now that you are hearing us, you want us to go away."

"Why do you have to interrupt my sleep? Saints' voices coming out of scarves. Really?"

I sit up and retrieve the scarf from the foot of the bed.

"We are formless. We come to you through love."

I feel the love wash over me and hug the scarf tight. It's just a tangible representation. I feel the tightly woven fibers, making up the perfect whole of the scarf.

It's made the Camino before.

Why did Mary insist on my bringing the scarf to the Camino? There has to be a greater purpose. Maybe it has nothing to do with me.

"Or maybe it has everything to do with you?" the scarf says.

I wonder what Mary left at Cruz de Ferro. I admire her drive and tenacity. But I guess we all keep our burdens close.

Emily presents as an accomplished executive with a tech company, full of faith and direction. I saw her tear up once, but I wasn't about to pry.

And Jackie, sweet Jackie. Such strength, conviction, and a huge heart. She's so comfortable in her skin. I hurt for her, the struggle with breast cancer, and her concern about her daughter.

Sister, a woman totally secure in her faith and her purpose. She lives her purpose every day.

Camille. She lost her husband at a young age. I'm sure she has struggled with some pretty heavy burdens and probably hasn't shared half of it. I don't know if I could have managed.

And Aino? I smile as I think about her. Another very accomplished woman with solid convictions. She and Camille are polar opposites.

I am so blessed with Ken and the kids. I really don't have anything to complain about. I'm not burdened.

Where do I stand on the issue of faith and the church? Are they different? I always thought they were the same thing. Will I go back to the church and simply be a housewife like I was before this trip, but more content in my role? I know I will fill my afternoons with something more than wine and card games. Or will I pursue a career?

I roll over again trying to find the elusive comfortable spot and tuck the scarf under my head again.

It is still dark when Sister gently shakes me awake. I didn't even realize I had slept. It feels like I've been awake all night. With an effort, I pull myself out of bed and make my way to the bathroom. I can see the lines of fatigue etched on my face in the mirror. My morning routine complete, I put my few belongings into my pack and join the group for a quick breakfast. Tossing and turning all night only accomplished exhaustion. This morning I release my burden and I still don't have a clue.

I wrap the scarf around my neck. "Yes you do," it says.

We put on our boots and shoulder our packs in silence. Each of us is lost in the significance of this dawn.

The sun is starting to peak over the horizon, as we approach the cross, The rocks and mementos placed at its foot create a man-made mountain. I wonder how many times the cross has been extended to soar above the sorrows at its foot. After the prayer, I hang back and watch as each person takes their turn at the cross. Some come off the mound with an incredible joy emanating from them. Some come off with their heads bowed in prayer. Some dance off, and some have tears rolling down their face. It's finally my turn. I've carried my stone all the way from Florida, so up to the cross I go.

'You know why you are here." The scarf whispering in my ear as I carefully pick my way up the mound.

I am aware I am treading on all the burdens that have previously been released with each step I take. The precious parts of people's lives through the ages. There are pictures of children, wedding rings, bits of ribbon, and pieces of paper with pilgrim prayers worn and faded by the weather. I steady myself on the stout wood pole that supports the iron cross twenty-five feet over my head.

"Helen, you are enough."

Tears well up in my eyes and run rivers down my face. I realize my burden is doubting myself, doubting the light that shines in me. Maybe this is where faith comes in.

I carefully place my stone of self-doubt, say a prayer of release, and make my way down the mound. A feeling of lightness and joy fills me. Sister points to the trail off the mountain. I carefully walk down the slick rocky path on the edge of the mountain. It wouldn't take much to slide off the edge.

Concentrating on where I put each foot and pole. I collide with a pilgrim who is standing still. I look up to apologize and see it is Aino. Tears are glistening on her cheek. Putting my arm around her waist, and she steadies herself by encircling mine. We gaze in silence at the incredible vista before us. The sun peeks out and a rainbow appears.

After a few moments, we release each other, turn, and continue to walk down the trail in silence towards Molinseca.

CHAPTER 24

MOLINESCA TO O'CEBREIRO TO SARRIA

The next couple of days are spent walking from Molinesca to O'Cebreiro. The terrain isn't easy. Up and down mountains and rugged trails. Concentration is imperative, so much of the time is spent in quiet reflection or muted conversation. I often find Aino close to me. Her presence is comforting.

The climb into the town of O'Cebreiro is breathtaking. At the top of the hill, a bronze statue of a female pilgrim is perched on a stone wall gazing out over the landscape. I stop to follow her gaze and to catch my breath. The plaque at the base, says she was created by Miguel Couto. Playfully I wrap the scarf around her neck. The rest of the group joins us, and we take turns posing with the stature and taking pictures.

"Look at those houses," Hannah says. "They must have quarried the rocks right here and thatched the roof with the hay from the fields. So, dope."

Behind a wall to our right is a small church, Santa Sophia La Real. This is where the miracle occurred that put O'Cebreiro on the map. Sister tells us about a poor farmer who walked through a horrible snowstorm to attend mass. He was the only parishioner who made the trip that day. The priest was roused out of his nice warm house to say Mass. The priest was not very happy and wanted to take it out on this faithful man. But he performed his duty. When he reached for the wafer and wine, it had transformed into flesh and blood. The priest was humbled by his lack of faith and begged forgiveness.

The albergue is over a shop that sells souvenirs. Tourists are sitting at small tables in front of the shop drinking wine and eating Caldo Gallego. We put a couple of tables together and order this famous soup. "It is made of beans, turnips greens, chorizo, salted pork, and spices. It is the specialty of Galicia," Sister says.

We enter the albergue quickly shower and do laundry. We have this down to a science. Then it is time to go to Mass.

The small church is alight with red votives placed on the floor in the shape of an arrow pointing to the altar. The priest motions to us to take a seat in the front pew. Hannah sits next to me. I smile and take her hand. The priest says Mass in both Spanish and English. Afterward, he invites us up to the altar for a special pilgrim blessing. Two local ladies hand out loaves of freshly baked bread. This will be delicious for breakfast.

I've reaped so much more than I would've believed, I thought, making my way to the albergue. I'm not ready for this to end. How will this experience change my life change when I return home? Will I easily slide back into my role as a mother and wife and be satisfied?

"Have faith," says the scarf.

Early the next morning, Aino and I leave the albergue together and head down the mountain. The path is rocky, and the high meadows are just starting to bloom. We stop to take in the beauty surrounding us. Aino takes my hand as we stand in silence. I look into her eyes and feel the love pouring out towards me. I respond with my mine. In silent communication, we share a love for each other.

She gently reaches for the scarf around my neck and pulls me forward into an embrace. I lift my face to hers. Her lips find mine. A warmth spreads down through my body and lights a fire in my groin. I find myself kissing her back and the flame flares. My body taking over, presses into hers. I can feel her breasts responding. She presses back as the kiss deepens.

Her hand makes its way down my back and cups the curve of my bottom. Coming back into my body I push her away, rip the scarf out of her hand, and run. I want to release it and let it fly over the edge of the mountain, but my fingers will not let go. Instead, I bring it to my face and let it soak up the tears. I stop, just short of the edge of a cliff. The cold wind coming off the peak of O'Cebreiro cools my passion.

How did I get here, so far from home and all that I know? I hear some of the others calling my name, but I'm not ready for them to find me. The kiss has left me trembling. I've never experienced anything like this in my forty-two years on this earth. I'm a mother of three and a wife of twenty years. Yet, none of that prepared me for the impact of that kiss.

"Mom!"

"Helen!"

They are calling. I just can't let Hannah see this turmoil.

I bury my face in the scarf. Hannah only knows me as Mom, loyal wife, kisser of cuts and scrapes. She doesn't know me as a passionate woman. She is so young, only eighteen, starting a new life. She needs me to be her rock right now.

"I am here for you," whispers the scarf.

I hear them coming around the corner. I quickly wipe my face with the scarf, so they won't know I have been crying. They will not see my weakness.

"Oh Mom, there you are. I was so afraid. Didn't you hear me calling? You and Aino were ahead of us, and I saw you push her away and run. Are you alright?"

"Yes, Hannah, I'm fine. I just needed some time to myself. It's so beautiful here."

Camille joins us, breathless. "Helen, I saw what happened and I saw Hannah coming up the trail behind me. I tried to protect her. She saw you run, and I said I would help her find you."

"Thank you, but there's nothing to worry about." I feel my words rushing out of me, so I slow their tempo. I need to act like nothing out of the ordinary has happened. "I just needed to lose myself in the view, put perspective on this pilgrimage, see where I came from. Let's head on down the trail. It's getting late, and we need to get to Triacastela. I can't believe that in less than a week we will be in Santiago. If you had told me when we first heard Sister talk at our home church in Tampa that I would have walked five hundred miles to Santiago, I would've laughed at you. Yet here we are, almost finished with our pilgrimage. And then, Hannah, you are off to college and your own life adventure."

"Hey Mom, don't rush it. I'm so glad we've had this time together. It's something I will always treasure."

"Yes, Helen, you're making wonderful memories for you and your family," Camille says, but I detect the sarcasm in her voice.

"Camille," I say getting a hold of myself. "Please excuse us. I need to talk to Hannah alone?"

"I guess you have some explaining to do. I will see you all in Triacastela." And she takes off down the trail alone.

"Mom, what did she mean?"

"I'm so ashamed. I have let a relationship go further than I expected, and I'm not sure where to go from here."

"Is it Aino?"

"Yes, how did you know?"

"Well, anyone could see the energy between you two. What happened?"

"I won't go into details, but we shared a kiss, and it shocked me. I don't want to hurt you, Dad, or the boys. It's over. I didn't expect our friendship to develop into something romantic. Having a relationship with Aino would be adultery, and I cannot commit adultery."

"Have you ever been attracted to women before?"

"No. It's just a misunderstanding. Your father and I are comfortable and committed. I just want you to know that. I'm not about to go running off to Afghanistan with Aino."

"I know, Mom."

We make our way down the path. I slow down and become lost in my thoughts. Hannah gets ahead of me. I wonder what she's thinking.

Looking at the scarf, I relive the memory of the kiss and the response of my body. I can feel the rush of blood overcome me. "Can I walk away from Aino like it never happened?" I ask myself.

She has been such a special friend, but I have only known her for a few weeks. It's like she's opened up a door I never knew existed. Have I been denying myself sexual feelings for so long that I forgot they were a part of me? Did it take a woman to wake them up?

Am I a lesbian?

I wonder how the boys and Ken will take this news. Or if I should even tell them. Will Ken be able to look at me and know something is different?

Hannah said she could see it before I even knew it was there. She wasn't surprised. She sure surprised me in her acceptance. I know this younger generation has had so much more experience with these things. Divorce and coming out is not something we ever discussed at home. It doesn't fit our doctrine. I've wondered at times about my lack of desire for sex. Deluding myself into believing that this is what nice women experience.

I haven't talked about it much with my girlfriends. We're too busy talking about children and recipes, not about sex. And we certainly don't associate with 'loose' women. Am I now a loose woman playing both sides of the fence?

This experience with Aino feels different than my experience with Ken. Throbbing, alive. I didn't know I could respond to a woman. Aino said she saw a light that needed to burst out and come into its own. Is this what she was talking about, sexual passion? In my innocence, I was thinking about my potential as a career woman. But as Jackie says there are many colors.

Am I more than just black or white?

"What do you think?" I say to the scarf.

"You are vibrant."

I hurry to catch up with Hannah, not wanting her to be alone.

It is late when we arrive in Triacastela.

The rest of the group has already showered. Sister encourages Hannah and me to get cleaned up so we can add our clothes to the communal washing machine. A real washing machine and dryer. What a luxury.

Once we shower, we gather in the foyer of the albergue

and go next door for dinner. Aino is missing. I pull Sister aside and ask her if she's seen her. She tells me she hasn't but that it's not unusual for pilgrims to take quiet time for themselves after Cruz de Ferro. I don't think this is the only reason Aino is missing.

The next day, we take an alternate route and make our way to Samos. There is a monastery there. Sister tells us that it was founded in the 6th century and has continued to be active all this time. Hannah is going to love this, living history.

After a night in Samos, we head toward Sarria.

I can't get that kiss out of my mind. And wonder if she feels the same way.

As we walk into Sarria, I find myself looking in the cafes with tables full of pilgrims searching for Aino among them. But I don't see her.

The church says, if a pilgrim successfully walks the last one hundred kilometers into Santiago, they qualify for a Compostela and absolution of their sins. I'm not sure one hundred kilometers is going to do it for me.

There's a large group of American college-aged kids standing in front of the church of Santa Marina. They must just be starting their Camino. Their boots and clothes look so clean. An older gentleman with a straw hat and grey beard soon gets them quieted down. I stop to listen. He is briefing them on the Camino, the logistics, and the rules for their adventure. I smile at their excitement. Hannah joins me to eavesdrop. A young man comes over to us after the lecture and introduces himself as Jose from the University of Miami. He tells us the group is walking the Camino as part of their Spanish cultural studies curriculum.

Hannah brightens as she tells him of some our experiences. He, in turn, tells her more about the University. I see the wheels turning, along with something else in her face. There's dangerous chemistry in the way she looks at him.

When the college group disperses, we get separated. As I'm looking for Hannah, the professor comes over and introduces himself. When he finds out we started in St. Jean he asks if we can join his group for wine and tapas at six pm and share our experiences. We exchange numbers. I say I will call him as I need to clear it with Sister. I catch a glimpse of Hannah's pack and hurry to catch up with her. She's walking next to the tall young man from Miami.

I quietly hang behind them, nonchalantly adjusting the scarf around my neck while I eavesdrop on the conversation. Their conversation is quite boring, all about the Camino and Spanish History. I should be ashamed of myself. Hannah is not doing anything out of line. I'm the one who's been out of line.

Later, after tapas with the students, Hannah asks if she can stay with the group a bit longer. I agree and make my way to our albergue and crawl into my bottom bunk. The familiar site of Aino sleeping in a bunk beside me is missing. I hadn't realized how much her presence had meant to me.

My 'mother alarm' goes off at about three am. I get up to make sure Hannah is safe in her bunk above me, but I find it empty. Her sleeping bag has not been rolled out. I check my phone. Has she been trying to text me? There's nothing. I text her and wait for a response. After five minutes I wake up Sister Sophia to let her know Hannah has disappeared.

Sister is not too concerned. "Sometimes young people stay out all night and show up in the morning."

I'm not having any of that and insist on going to the police. Harm could have come to my daughter. Ken would never forgive me. I would never forgive myself.

Sister puts her hands on my shoulders, trying to calm me. "The police are familiar with young people staying out all night and they won't do anything until morning."

I'm beside myself. Sister gives me directions to the police station and tells me she will stay at the albergue in case Hannah comes back. I march to the door of the albergue and discover that it's locked. What if Hannah is sitting outside and can't get in? But, she would have called me. I turn the deadbolt and let myself out. She's not on the stoop.

I make my way down the street to the police station. There's a sleepy young officer on duty. He doesn't speak much English, but I get the message across that my daughter is missing. He just looks at me, shrugs, and says not to worry. She will return. "It is very safe, and no harm will come to her. Go back to bed."

My phone dings with a text message from Hannah. *I'm fine, with students, CU in the am.*

I feel the heat of embarrassment rush to my face.

The police officer cocks his head and gestures to my phone. *"¿Todo está bien?"*

Yes, all is well. I thank him, then make my way back to the albergue, trying to decide how I'm going to ground her in Spain.

Sister is waiting up for me. Her expression tells me that she must see the relief and anger on my face. She says that this part of Spain is not like living in a city. It's safe, and young people have been known to want to experience life on their own.

Well, not on my watch.

Hannah gets to the albergue just as our group is getting ready to leave.

"Get your pack and let's go. We need to talk," I tell her, barely able to contain my anger. She quickly packs and follows me out into the street.

I point my finger right at her face. "Young lady, what do you mean by staying out all night and scaring me half to death? You not only kept me awake, but you kept Sister awake too. I even went to the police station to make a missing person's report."

"Oh Mom, I'm so sorry. I thought you knew where I was."

"Well, the last I knew you were hanging around with that young college guy, if that's really who he is."

"I wasn't with just him, but the whole group. There were girls there, too. They kept asking me about the Camino and my experiences, and I kept asking them about college. Before I knew it we had talked half the night. We fell asleep. I had my own bunk."

"I saw the look in his eyes when he was talking to you. You are too young to know what men his age really want from a girl. We're halfway around the world and you don't even speak the language. What if they had kidnapped you, or worse?"

"Mom, that's a little dramatic." Hannah starts to give me her famous eye roll but catches herself.

"I need to know I can trust you. You know what your curfew is."

"This is not home, and we didn't discuss a curfew on this trip."

"Just because we aren't home doesn't give you license

to stay out all night. What is your father going to say about this?"

"Well, at least I didn't kiss anyone."

The words reach across the space between us and slap me hard across the face. I'm stunned. There's a moment of silence, then she snatches the scarf from around my neck, turns, and walks away.

CHAPTER 25

PORTOMARÍN TO AMENAL

I was told it was a downhill run from here to Santiago. They were lying. I trudge up yet another short hill and carefully make my way down the other side only to start uphill again. Wouldn't it have been easier to make this all flat?

At last, the river comes into view. A huge bridge spans the Minho River. Once across the river, I will be in Portomarín with less than a week to go to Santiago. It is time to go home. I have had enough of this Camino.

The pilgrims ahead of me are crossing. I see Hannah's pack in among a small group of pilgrims. They don't look like our group. She must've joined the college kids.

I am alone as I cross the bridge, but it can't be too hard to find our albergue. Sister said we had reservations at Ultreia, a small private albergue just past the center of town.

I come to a standstill at the foot of a huge staircase. I look for a yellow arrow to point me in a different direction but can't find one. There are sidewalks along the main roads, but no arrows.

Someone behind me says *"Perdon"*.

I move to the side to let a group of young pilgrims up the stairs. They are talking and laughing as they mount the steps. This must be the way. Oh my.

I start up the staircase. The steps are narrow and close together. The climb is perilous. A cold sweat breaks out. I could die or worse if I fall. Finally, I reach the arch at the top of the steps and walk through it, only to find another shorter flight up to the street. Will this never end?

I follow the arrows into town. They make a sharp left turn and start back toward the river. There must be something wrong here. I get out my guidebook and map. The way continues back down and across another bridge, but we are staying in town. A gentleman walks up and asks me if I need assistance. He must be able to tell that I am a lost, disoriented pilgrim. I give him the name of the albergue, and he graciously leads me there.

Camille calls to me when I enter. "Helen, there you are. We were starting to get worried."

"So was I, but a nice gentleman showed me where to go. Where is everyone?"

"Emily and Sister are working on a letter to give to dioceses about expanding the role of women in the church.

And Jackie and Hannah are with the college students. At least I know where your daughter is. I am glad it is just us; we need to talk."

"All right, do you want to talk now, or may I shower first?" I say, not that I need her permission.

"Now is fine. I'm very concerned about Hannah. She's young and impressionable, and your traipsing around with Aino has just confused and upset her. I know she didn't come back to the albergue last night. You need to pay more attention to your daughter and less attention to Aino."

I'm astounded at her audacity. "I don't think this is any of your business."

"And another thing. You, a married woman, pursuing a relationship with another woman is still adultery in my book. What is this going to do to your husband and your children? You know you can go to hell for this kind of behavior."

I shake my head in amazement. "Just a minute here..."

She steps closer and wags a finger in my face. "No, you need to hear this. You're ruining your life, and no one has the guts to stand up to you. I see through your act of being the perfect mother and nurse. You're not fooling me or anyone else."

"What I do is between myself, God, and whoever else I choose to be on the list And are not on it." I point a finger back at her. "I don't have to stand here and be judged by you." I turn, open my pack, and start pulling out my clean clothes and toiletries.

"This is for your own good. You are going down the road of self-destruction and I'm not going to stand by and watch it."

"You don't have to. I didn't ask you to be my judge. Maybe you should put some of that energy into looking at your own behavior." I flip open my small pack-towel.

"How dare you try to turn the tables on me. I am not the one cheating on my husband or letting my daughter run wild."

"Excuse me, I'm going to go take my shower now." I nudge her aside and head to the bathroom. "That bitch. No wonder people are leaving the church," I murmur, hoping she didn't see the tears trying to run down my face.

She has no clue. She does not deserve the glory of knowing she made me cry. I've only been kind and supportive of her. How dare she? How dare I? How did I lose control of my life? I didn't intend to cheat on my husband or lose my temper with Hannah.

In the shower, I let the warm water run over me and wash away the dirt and tears. I don't want to get out and face anyone in the group. I've made a mess of things.

I finish up and head to the laundry sink, where I wash my clothes and hang them on the line. I don't know where Camille went, and I don't care as long as she stays away from me. Back in the bunk room, I roll out my sleeping bag and lie down. The next thing I know, Hannah is shaking me awake.

"Mom, Mom, wake up. Are you alright?" she says.

"What time is it?" I roll over, rubbing my eyes.

"It's seven and it's time to get on the road. We have twenty-five klicks to Palas de Rei."

I shake my head in an attempt to clear it. "What about dinner?"

"It's seven in the morning. Camille said you were exhausted and were not going to join us for dinner. So, we just let you sleep."

I can't believe I slept for so long. "Wow, I must've been exhausted."

She sits on the side of the bunk and grabs my hand. "Mom, I'm so sorry for staying out all night and causing you so much worry."

My daughter's face is full of remorse, and tears are beginning to run down her cheeks. I take the end of the scarf that is now around her neck and blot her face with it. "Thank you. I was young once and would lose track of time." I pull her to me. "I was just so scared; I don't want anything to happen to you."

"I know Mom. *Vamos*. We have places to go and people to see!" She hands me my clean clothes.

Are you walking with the college crowd today?' I say, pulling on my pants and socks.

"Well, I hope to meet up with them. It's so interesting learning about the history and the culture of the area from the professor."

"And is Jose interesting, too?" I fumble with the button on my shirt. Hannah knocks my hand away and does it for me.

"Yes, he's a really nice man. I'd like you to get to know him a little."

"Let's see if we can catch up with them." I shoulder my pack and we make our way out the door. "By the way, the scarf suits you."

"Agreed," the scarf says.

The town cafe is the first thing I see as we walk into Gonzar. They sure know how to welcome pilgrims. The students call to Hannah and me to join them. They have cleared a seat for her next to Jose. I take a seat next to the professor.

"I'm so sorry you were worried about your daughter. I thought she had permission to join us. If I'd known, I would've walked her back to your albergue myself," he says the minute I sit down.

"She told me she was with you all, but I didn't know she planned on a sleepover. All is well."

"I'm so glad. She is such a bright and curious young lady.

I would love to have her in my class. She said she's starting at the community college."

"That's right," I nod at him. What a relief, she is going to go to school and not traipse off around the world by herself, without a plan.

He continues, "When it comes time for her to further her studies. I would be pleased to recommend her."

"How generous of you." I start to touch his arm but immediately pull back my hand. I don't need any more trouble.

"She deserves it. In Spain, a young person can put walking the Camino on their resume, and it speaks volumes of their character. Unfortunately, we don't have a similar system in the U.S. I see a lot of young people, and, after a while, you learn to pick out the ones with potential. That daughter of yours has potential."

"I'm proud of her. She works hard and has such passion for life."

The waiter comes by to take my order. I'm starving. *"Tortilla de patatas* and a *café con leche,* por favor," Reaching for the basket in the center of the table, I pull out a slice of soft, still-warm bread and slather butter all over it.

My egg and potato omelet comes quickly, and I dive in, aware I have a long day ahead. Finished, I pay for our breakfast and begin to look for the next yellow arrow. Jose joins me and Hannah. We walk in a quiet, easy way.

Sometimes talking, sometimes in silence.

I feel the energy of the pilgrims of the past pulling me along. The feeling gets stronger as we get closer to Santiago. I no longer need a guide.

I miss Aino and wonder what happened to her. I reacted so badly to the kiss. She really took a risk. Maybe I'm not the victim. Maybe I've victimized her. She must have picked up signals that I was interested in more than friendship. Maybe I am. I don't know.

On the bright side, I have enjoyed getting to know young Jose a little bit better. I'm half afraid this is a vacation fling. I don't want Hannah to get hurt, but it's also nice to see her enjoying the company of such a sharp young man. Hannah hasn't repeated the disappearing act either. She's been careful to let me know where she is.

We arrive at the hotel in Amenal and gather in the dining room. As we take our seats at the table, Sister and Emily pass around the rough draft of the letter they wrote to the College of Bishops about women's roles in the church.

It reads as follows:

Dear _____

Women have been an integral part of the church for millennia. The Virgin Mary brought Christ onto the Earth plane. The role of women should not stop with being just vessels for creation and nurturing. Women can use these and their other gifts to further the mission of the church to bring all to Christ.

Women and men have been one, and this partnership only strengthens us. Women who have the talent to preach, pray, administer, and serve should be allowed to do so in the same roles as their male counterparts, should it be as a priest, bishop, archbishop, cardinal or pope. St. Paul wrote in his letter to the Galatians 3:26-28 "Through faith you are all children of God in Christ Jesus. For all of you who were baptized into Christ have clothed yourselves with Christ. There is neither Jew nor Greek, there is neither slave nor free person, there is not male and female; for you are all one in Christ Jesus."

Yet the Code of Canon Law #1024 only allows men to hold these roles. This is a law made by men, not by God. Men can change this law to be inclusive. The discrimination against a woman taking any of these roles is not congruent with the word of Christ.

The Church has made public its view on discrimination with Vatican II, Pastoral Constitution on the Church in the Modern World, #29 "Forms of social or cultural discrimination in basic personal rights on the grounds of sex, race, color, social conditions, language or religion must be curbed and eradicated as incompatible with God's design."

Please join us in presenting our petition to change Canon Law #1024 and allow women to be equal to men in aspiring to take any role for which they have the talent and desire in the church.

Camille tosses her copy onto the center of the table. "Blasphemy."

Emily turns to her and quietly says, "No, this is the truth. Are you calling St. Paul a heretic?"

"No, of course not. But tradition is so important. If you change the order of things, there will be chaos. People will start behaving unnaturally." She turns to me as she says this. Then she looks at everyone in turn before she zeroes in on Hannah. "Do you understand what I am saying?"

"Camille," Jackie interjects. "What makes it so important to you to lash out at Helen?"

"Helen must understand what she's doing to her child.

Her child has the most to lose in this situation. She needs a strong Christian role model. She's been running wild with you and Helen has allowed it."

Jackie nearly spits out the sip of water she's just taken. "Don't even attempt to tarnish my reputation or Hannah's. You have no idea what you're saying. What are you so afraid of?"

Camille's anger deflates as sadness moves up through her heaving chest. When she starts to cry, Jackie leans over and envelopes her in a hug.

"I have lost so much," Camille says through her sobs. "I cannot lose my faith too. The church is where I get my strength and you all are taking it away."

"No, honey, we're making it stronger." Jackie leans back and looks into Camille's eyes. "Faith is like a stool, and it can't stand on two legs. I see God as one leg, man as the other, and women as the third. We're losing our women by denying them a leadership role in the church. This will bring balance. Have you ever aspired to do more for the church than your role has allowed?"

"No, never. I was brought up to know my place," Camille tells her.

Emily speaks up. "You mean the place of doing whatever men asked you to do without question, whether it was right or wrong?"

A blush creeps up Camille's face and she turns her head away from the group.

"Well?" Emily insists.

"I made a mistake once of putting a man before God. At church the following Sunday the priest talked about the importance of remaining chase until marriage. I knew he was talking to me. I knew I had sinned. I went to confession, and he gave me a very difficult penance to cleanse my soul." Camille digs out a tissue and blows her nose. "The thing was, John had just been accepted to college and we were going to wait until he graduated to get married. But we couldn't control our passion. A couple of months later, I realized I was pregnant. John agreed to marry me, give up his future at college, and he took a job at the local drug store. We struggled, but somehow, we made ends meet. I had to take a job after our second child came along. But I knew the church would look down on us if we used birth control."

"I'm so sorry you had no choice in that," Emily says.

"Choice? I chose to have my children. When I got pregnant the third time with my little girl, the doctor said she wasn't viable, but I chose to have her anyway. There was no way I was going to abort her. But God took her home before she drew a breath. My little angel." Camille is crying again.

"I'm so sorry," Jackie grabs her hand and squeezes it.

Camille shakes her head to get control and smiles, "but then He gave us two more fine boys. God knew what he was doing. We should not question it."

"When John died and left me alone, the church didn't desert me. Father Tim was there for me and the children. He has been my strength and refuge, and you're trying to take this away."

Jackie hasn't let go of Camille's hand, and now she puts an arm around her. "I'm so sorry you had to go through all this. I understand why you feel it's important to teach young women values and to find comfort in the church."

"Camille," I say. "I've been so selfish, thinking of me and what I want, when you have been suffering. I am sorry for any pain I have caused you."

Camille pulls away from Jackie and turns to me. "You haven't caused me any pain. I'm trying to protect your daughter."

"I understand your need to protect but I, too, have faith and trust in God and my daughter."

The tears dry up. Standing, Camille slaps her hand down on the table. "Well, you have a funny way of showing it. There's no talking sense into any of you." She turns to Sister Sophia. "And I can't believe you're allowing this to happen."

Sister doesn't appear to take any offense to Camille's accusation. She takes a sip of her drink before answering. "I don't believe that allowing women to aspire to greater leadership roles in the church will add to its downfall. I believe it will only strengthen us. I know many will ridicule me for my belief, but there are just as many in the faith that will applaud me."

"So, they've brainwashed you too, Sister. Well, I will not turn against the church." That said, Camille stands and storms out of the room.

CHAPTER 26

SANTIAGO DE COMPOSTELA

The next morning, the alarm goes off at five o'clock. We want to make the sixteen-kilometer trek into Santiago in time for the noon mass at the Cathedral so that means an early start. The Camino continues to be a series of short ups and downs along asphalt roads by the airport. Then we get relief entering dirt paths with high banks on each side as they wander through incredible eucalyptus forests. The aroma coming from the trees is healing to my exhausted body.

We climb the last mountain, Mount de Gozo, the mountain of joy, overlooking the city. Standing at the summit we see the spires of the cathedral in the distance. We grab each other screaming and hugging. The spires of the cathedral are in view.

It takes forever to walk down the mountain and through the outskirts of the city. I can't believe I am going to make the entire five hundred miles. It seems like yesterday, and like forever, that I left St. Jean. I've only known these women for just over a month, yet it feels like a lifetime.

I know I've changed. I'm so glad Hannah and I are easy with each other. Heaven knows what I'm going to say to Ken. And Aino, I don't know what to think now that she has disappeared. I can easily make the feelings she stirred up within me disappear too.

We make our final approach to the cathedral. I feel the excitement through the ancient narrow, winding streets of Santiago. Each step brings me out of my thoughts and into the present. We walk into the Praza do Obradoiro, it is teeming with pilgrims, taking pictures, hugging each other, and celebrating their journey.

Hannah grabs me and we cling to each other. She gently takes one end of the scarf from around her neck and wraps it around mine, joining us together. The last time we were joined was when she was in the womb. The warmth from her body envelops mine. Our tears mix as our foreheads touch. This daughter of mine.

The scarf whispers, "You are enough. Pay attention to the possibilities. Nothing is out of reach."

EPILOGUE

The next morning, I got up and took a walk. The guidebook had said something about a church that was built in the 12th Century on swamp land just outside of town, called the Collegiate Church of Santa Maria a Real do Sar. In the 17th century, due to the instability of the ground, it started to lean and had to be supported to prevent it from falling down. This is my kind of place.

I walked into the nave and saw another pilgrim kneeling in quiet contemplation in a pew in front of the altar. Compared to all the churches I have been in; the simplicity was refreshing. It gave me room to breathe.

The altar was a simple block of stone, covered by a white cloth. There was a tall candlestick at each end of the altar, holding candles to light the way. Behind the altar, there was a small cubby with a door. This cubby held the eucharist. Mother Mary was above the altar, enveloping me in her light. Her eyes seemed to meet mine and it felt like the loving hug of a mother. No wonder the Catholics revere her.

Kneeling to pray, I chose a spot several pews back from

the pilgrim so that I didn't disturb the silence. Allowing myself to hear the voice that had been with me on the Camino, I caressed the scarf around my neck.

I am enough, I am a mother, a lover, a wife, a nurse, a friend. There is room for all.

I heard footsteps and looked up. A pilgrim was coming down the aisle towards me. It was Aino and there were tears on her face. I quietly stood and we walked together out of the nave to the river. We sat down on a bench and Aino broke the silence with an apology.

"I am so sorry to have kissed you. I misunderstood our relationship. I thought you wanted to be with me also."

"Oh Aino, you stirred up feelings in me I never knew existed. I ran out of fear. I'm not ready to make such a huge change in my life. I'm grateful that you kissed me. I never would have known that I had the potential to love like that."

"Helen, you have incredible potential. I saw it the moment I met you. It is your light that attracted me. I am here."

"I'm glad. Seeing you again confirms that I cannot pretend the feelings for you don't exist. But I'm not ready to run away with you to Afghanistan."

"Oh, I know that you have a family and a new career to consider. But I hope that you consider our relationship also."

"I will. I'll always remember what you have taught me. But I can't make any promises."

"I know. I just could not help myself. The pull of you is so strong. I saw you standing above that field of flowers with the scarf dancing in the breeze. It just danced into my hands, and I was lost. I had to kiss you, I had to know."

I took a deep breath. I had to know too. But it was too soon for me. I had to go home and see what I needed to hold onto and what I needed to release. I trusted myself to make the best decision for me. I knew I couldn't keep swaying with the breeze.

"You can love again Aino. Would you join us for our celebration dinner tonight? The Barrier Bust-ers have written a letter to the College of Bishops and we are going to map out our plan of changing the role of women in the church."

"Yes, I would like that very much."

Smiling, we stood and silently made our way back to Santiago.

The journey of the scarf continues in book two with Valerie, the maiden. She will dance into our lives in 2025. Keep reading for a sneak peek.

THE CAMIGAS SCARF
Dance like the Maiden: Book Two

VALERIE

"Helen, I'm never going to learn how to solve these dose calculation problems. They'll flunk me." I run my fingers through my braids replacing the scrunchy once again. I just have to make it through nursing school. It's been my dream since I was a little girl.

One of my earliest memories is being in the hospital. I couldn't breathe. This nice nurse put an oxygen mask on me and gave me a special blanket with 'Hello Kitty' on it. She said, '"The kitty will watch over you." I want to be that nurse.

"Oh Valerie, you are not going to flunk. Take a deep breath, exhale, and relax." I take a minute and Helen goes on. "There are a couple of ways to solve this intravenous drip-rate problem. Some people get it one way, some get it another. Let me show you a different way and see it that makes more sense."

"You are so patient with me. How can I ever thank you?"

"You helped me memorize all those medications and side

effects. It was one of the things that really worried me when I first thought about going back to nursing school," Helen says.

"Okay. Show me again how to solve this problem."

"No problem." Helen winks, "But we'll solve it together."

Coming up with an answer, I look at her for confirmation. "Yes, that's it, you have it now!"

"You're the best,"

"Thanks. Now, let's take a break and have some tea. Make yourself at home while I put the kettle on."

I wander from the dining room to the living room. A large frame containing some documents on the wall catches my attention. "Helen, what are the documents in this frame?"

"That's my Compostela and credential. When you walk the Camino de Santiago in Spain, you receive absolution from your sins, and they give you a document to prove it."

"You, a sinner?"

"Well, it's a long story," Helen says from the kitchen.

"I watched a movie at church called "I'll Push You" about a pilgrimage in Spain. I have been wanting to go ever since,"

"Yes, it is the same pilgrimage I did with Hannah before she went off to college. It was a mother-daughter trip and so much more. You should do it. It's life-changing."

"I don't know if I can do it. I was born with a hole in my heart. You know the ventricular septal defect. The doctors fixed it surgically when I was a baby, but sometimes I get short of breath. It feels like my heart is beating out of my chest. Mom still treats me like a baby, I doubt she'd be willing to let me go." I get closer to the frame to look at the stamps on her credential. I want one.

"Ask your doctor. But it's not a race. I tried to walk too fast at times and got into trouble. If you listen to your body and walk slowly, it shouldn't be a problem. Are you thinking about going after nursing school?"

"Well, I was thinking about this summer before we start our senior year."

"If you decide to go let me know. I'm happy to lend you any of my gear and provide any information you need," Helen says, maybe even the scarf.

"That would be great. It's so amazing. I just saw the movie, thought about going, and then met someone who's done it. What are the chances?"

But, I just have to get it past my mother. She's so overprotective. Ever since Dad died when I was six, it's just been the two of us. And with my medical problems, she has a hard time letting me go.

O'Cebreiro, Galicia

ALDER ALLENSWORTH

Alder Allensworth walked her first Camino in 2017. When she arrived in Burgos she was informed that the manuscript for her first book, Prevail: Celebrate the Journey, had won a contract with Richter Publishing. It was published in 2018.

She returned to the Camino in 2022 for a writer's retreat. This is where the book began to take shape. Serendipitously, the scarf made its way back to her. She took it to the top of O'Cebreiro to take the photo for the cover of this book.

She works as a nurse, but in her free time pursues her other passions. These include membership in the Tampa Writer's Alliance and a project to help children understand Alzheimer's disease. She and her partner, Brenda Freed, have published the Mackenzie Meets Alzheimer's Disease Picture Book and have created the Mackenzie Meets Alzheimer's Awareness Program. She is active with the American Pilgrims on the Camino and is a local chapter coordinator.

She lives in Tampa, Florida, and can be contacted through her website www.alderallensworth.com or directly by email at aldertree0720@gmail.com.